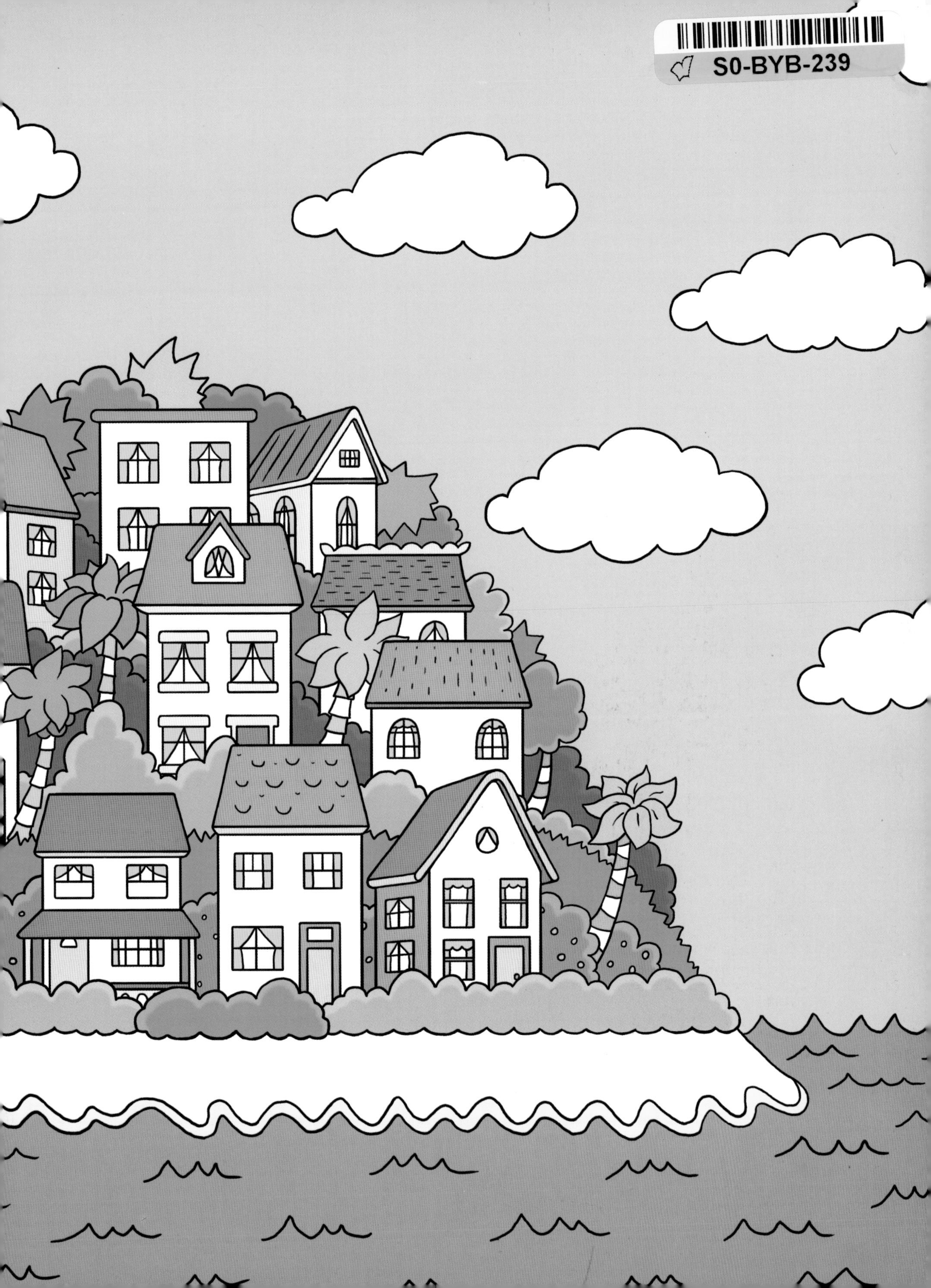

# MONKEY & ELEPHANT'S
## Worst Fight Ever!

# Michael Townsend

Alfred A. Knopf

One evening, Monkey set out to bring his best friend, Elephant, a surprise gift. . . .

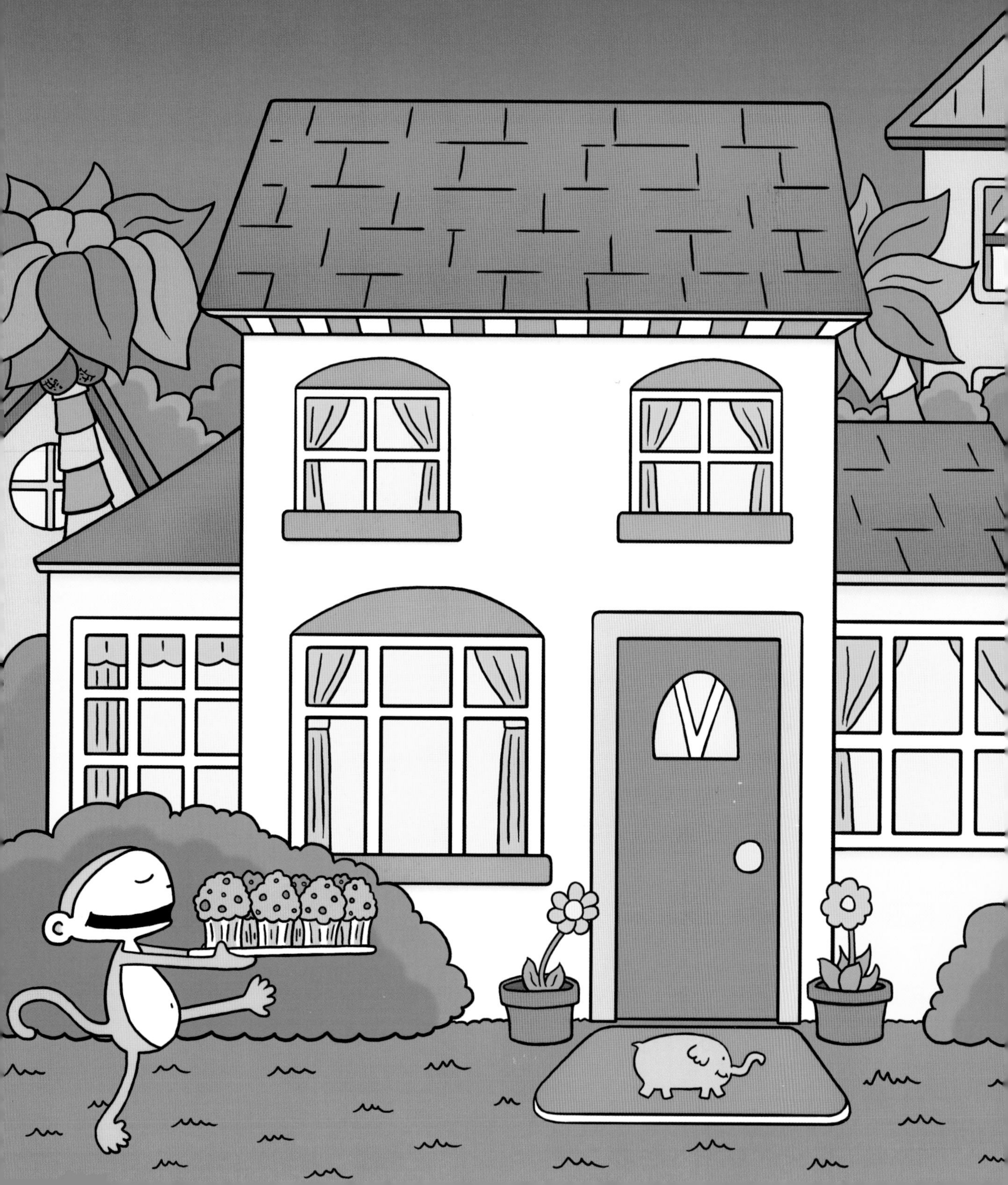

But before he could knock on the door, he saw something shocking.

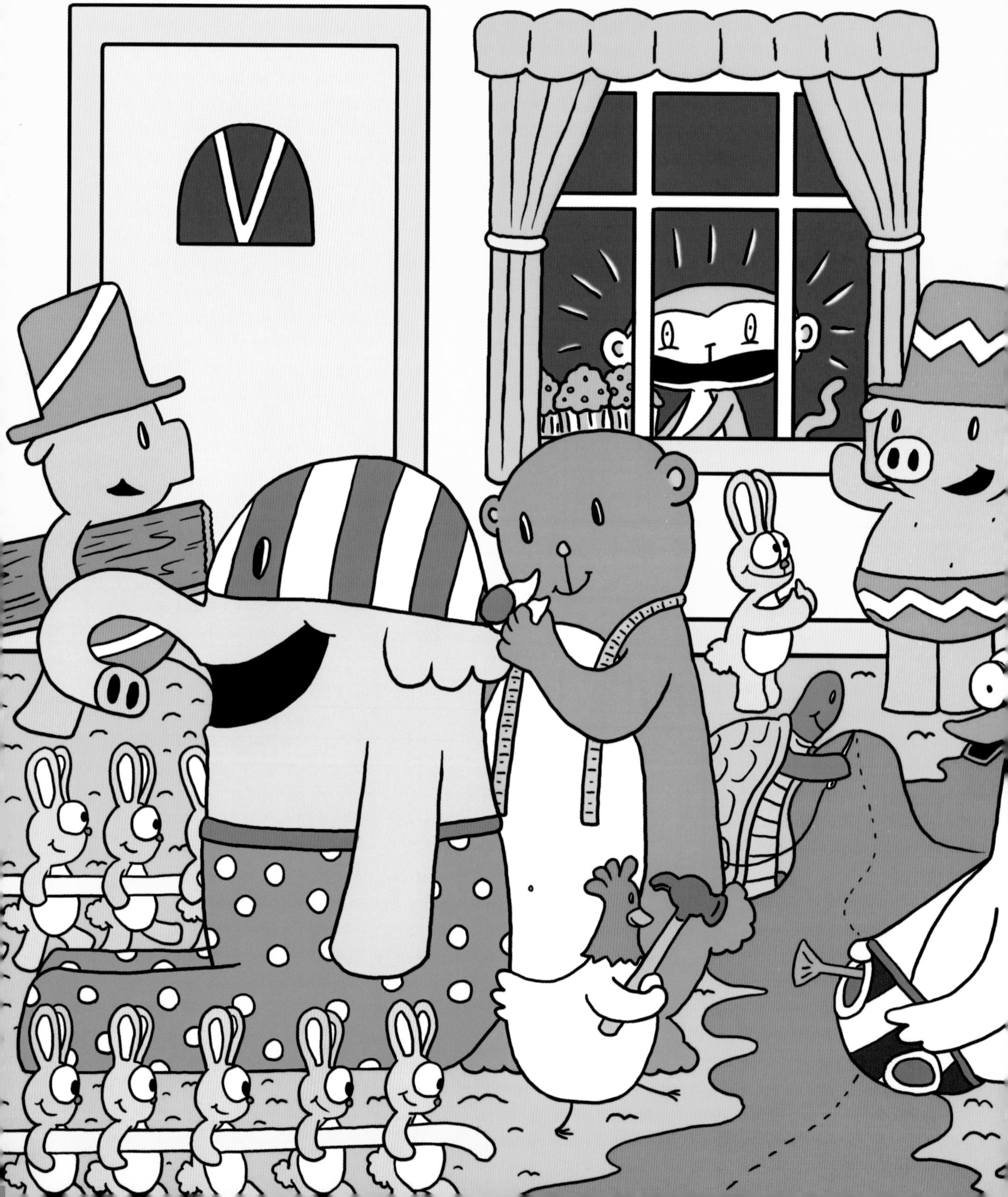

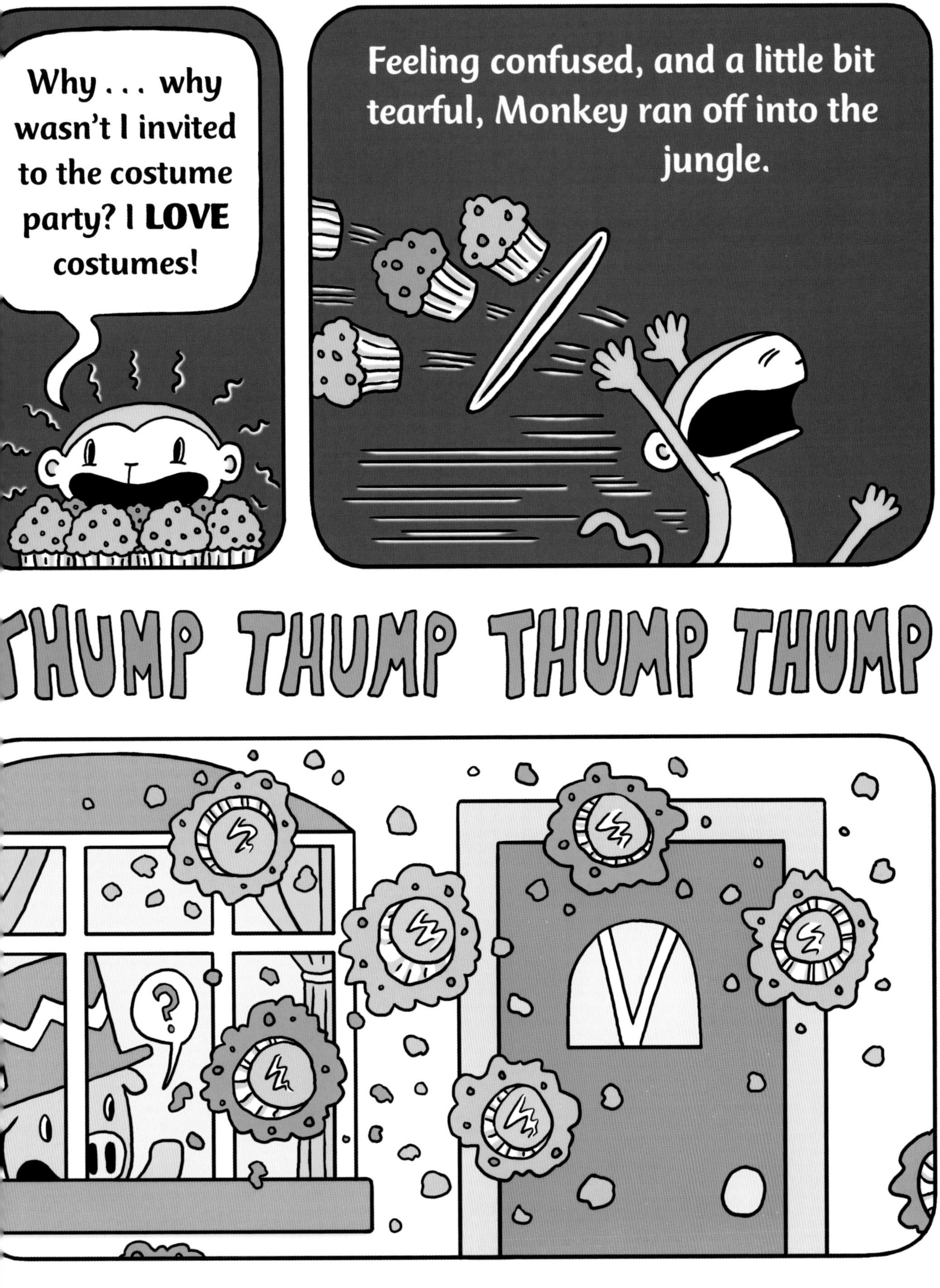
Why . . . why wasn't I invited to the costume party? I **LOVE** costumes!
Feeling confused, and a little bit tearful, Monkey ran off into the jungle.
THUMP THUMP THUMP THUMP
?

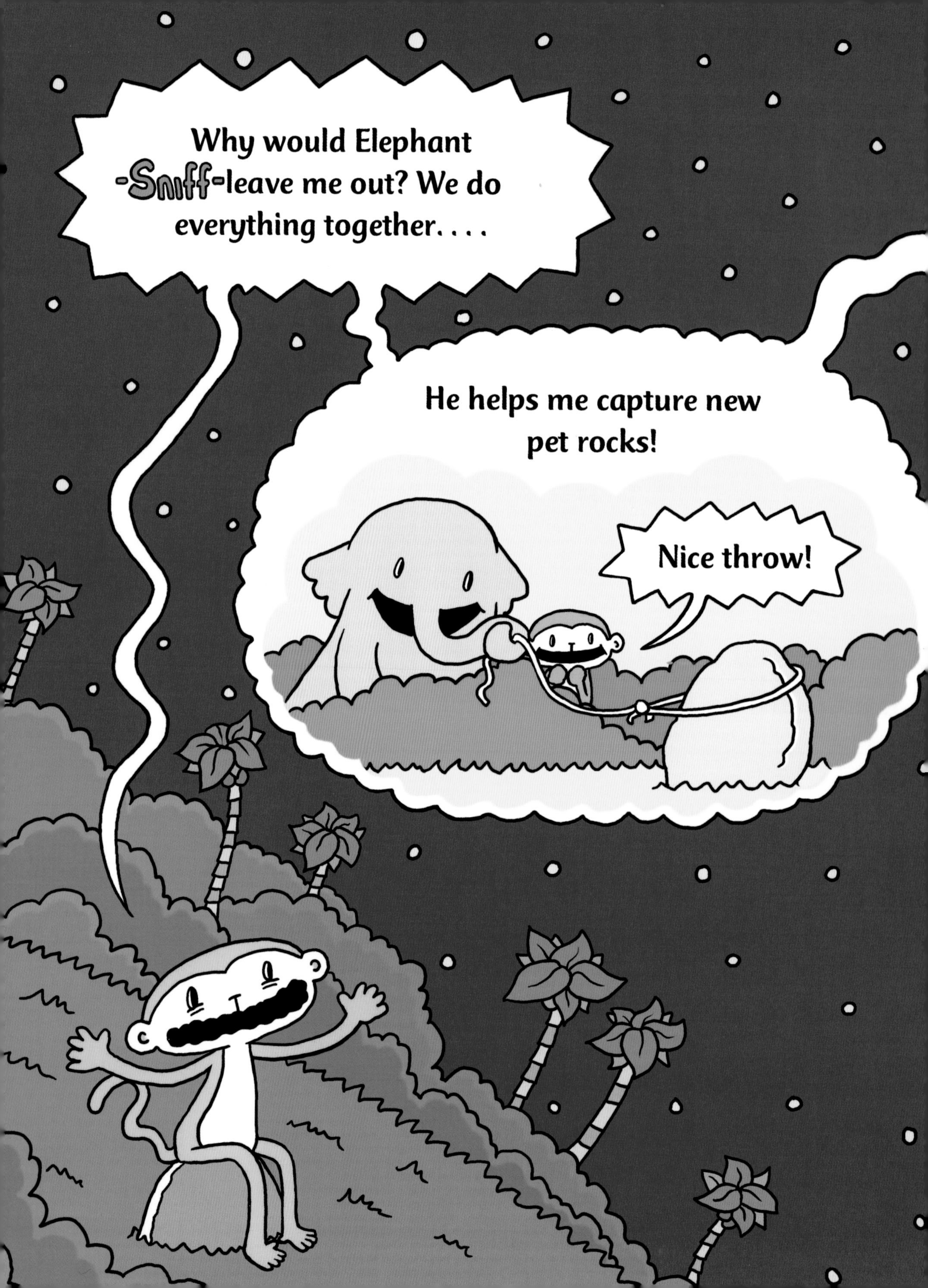
Why would Elephant -Sniff-leave me out? We do everything together. . . .
He helps me capture new pet rocks!
Nice throw!

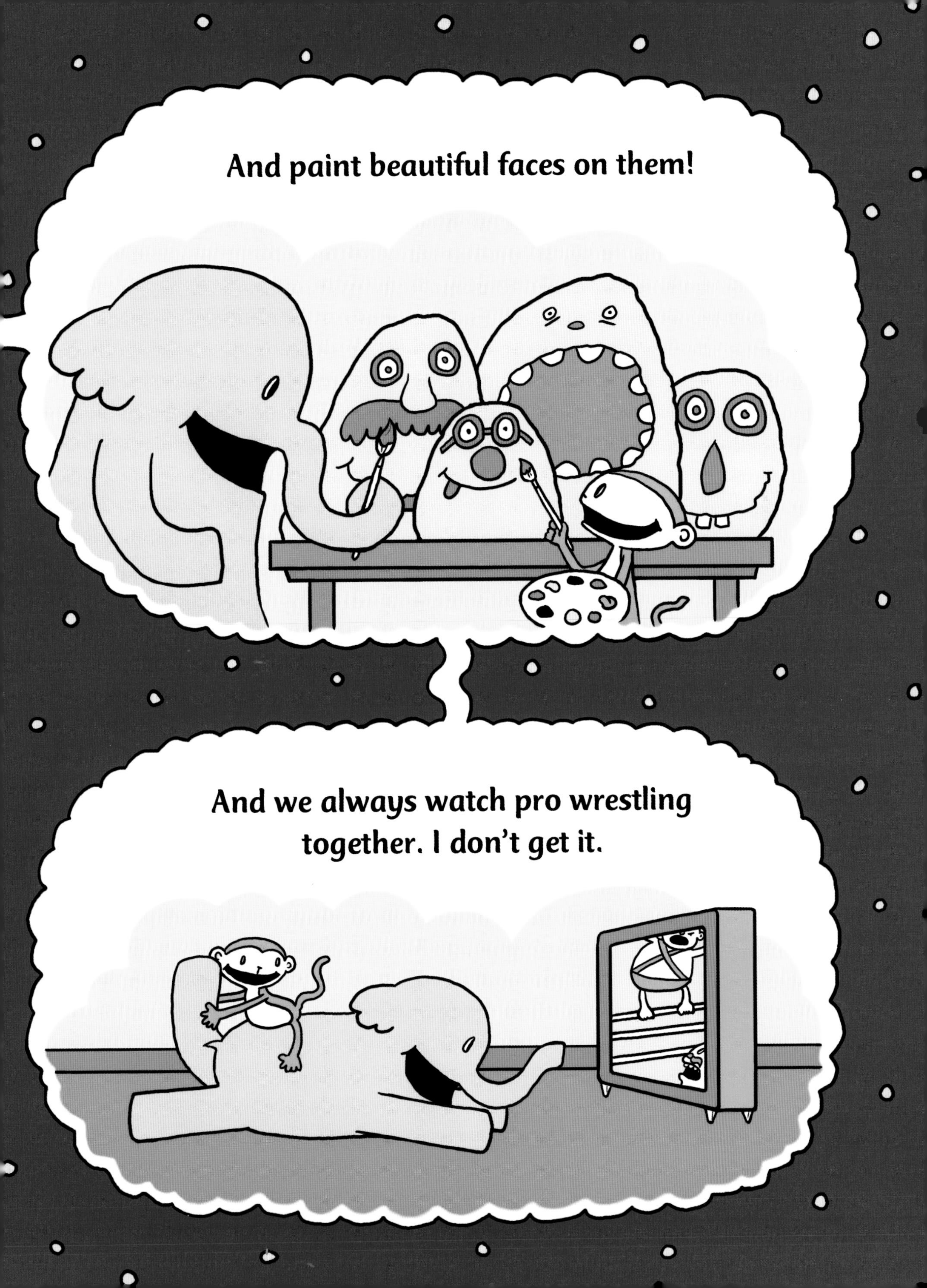
And paint beautiful faces on them!
And we always watch pro wrestling together. I don't get it.

Monkey quickly went from feeling sad...

SNIFF
SNIFF
GRRRR
SNIFF
GRRRR

...to feeling mad.

Monkey decided to get even.

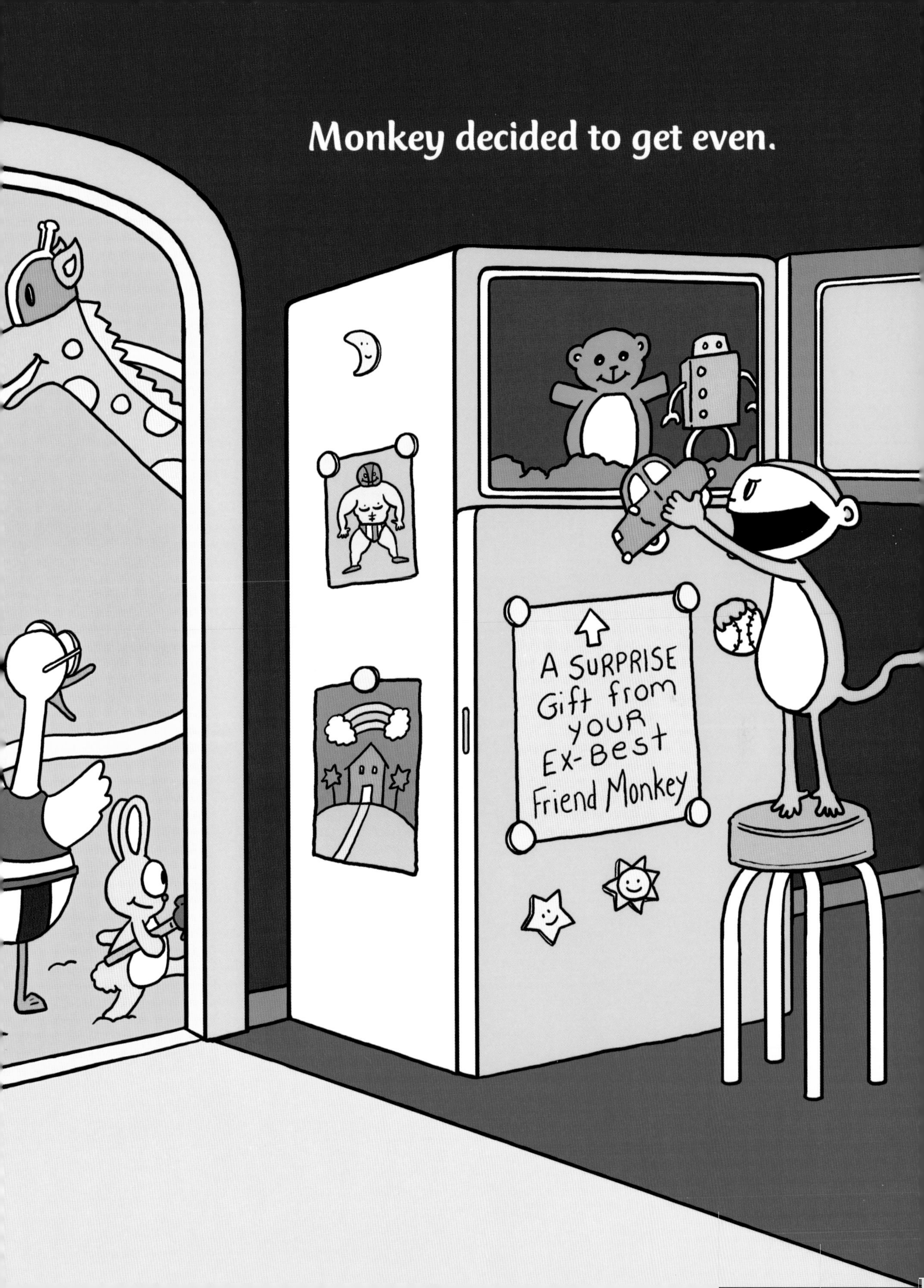
A SURPRISE Gift from YOUR Ex-Best Friend Monkey

The next morning, Elephant was shocked when he discovered what Monkey had done.

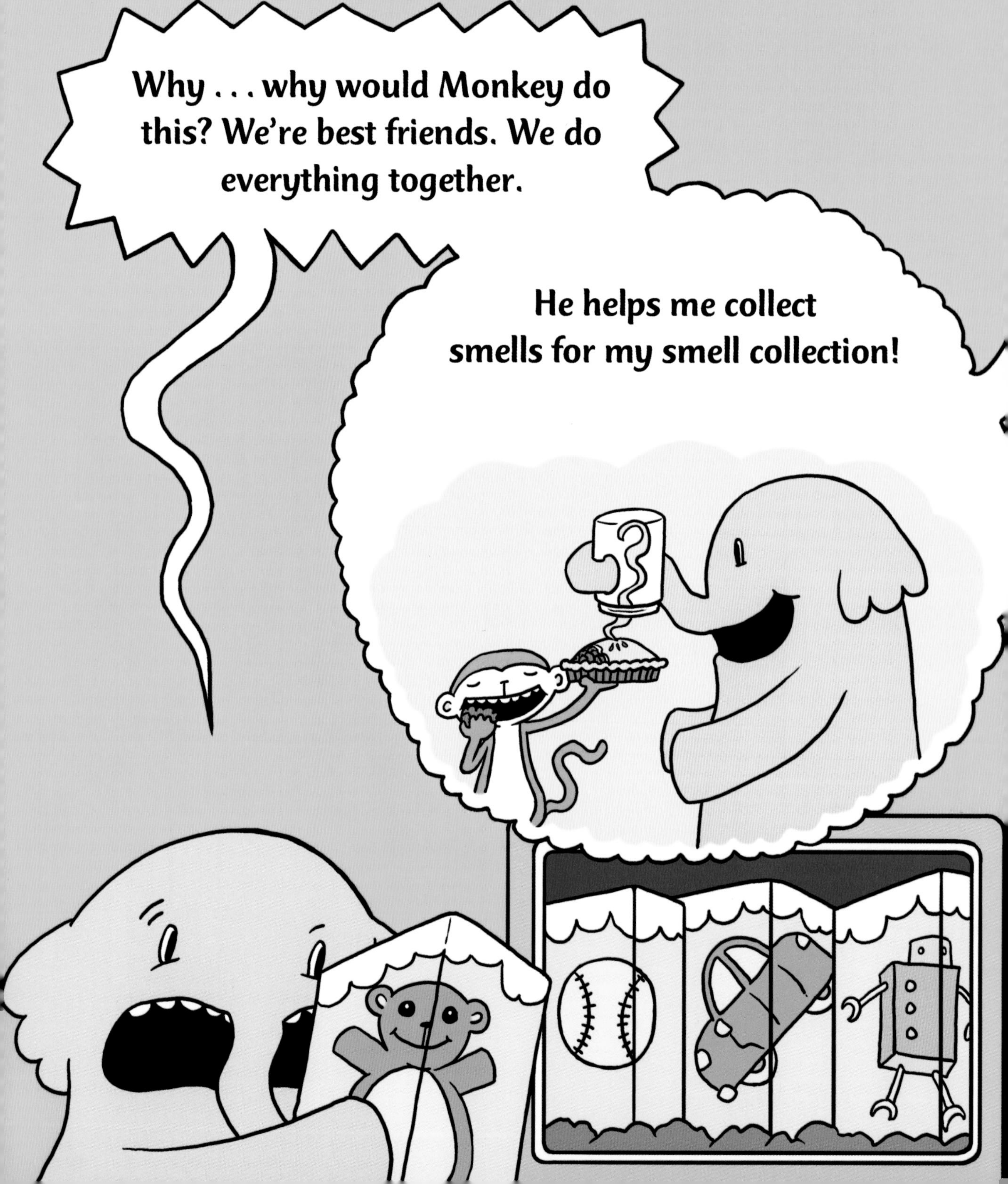
Why . . . why would Monkey do this? We're best friends. We do everything together.
He helps me collect smells for my smell collection!

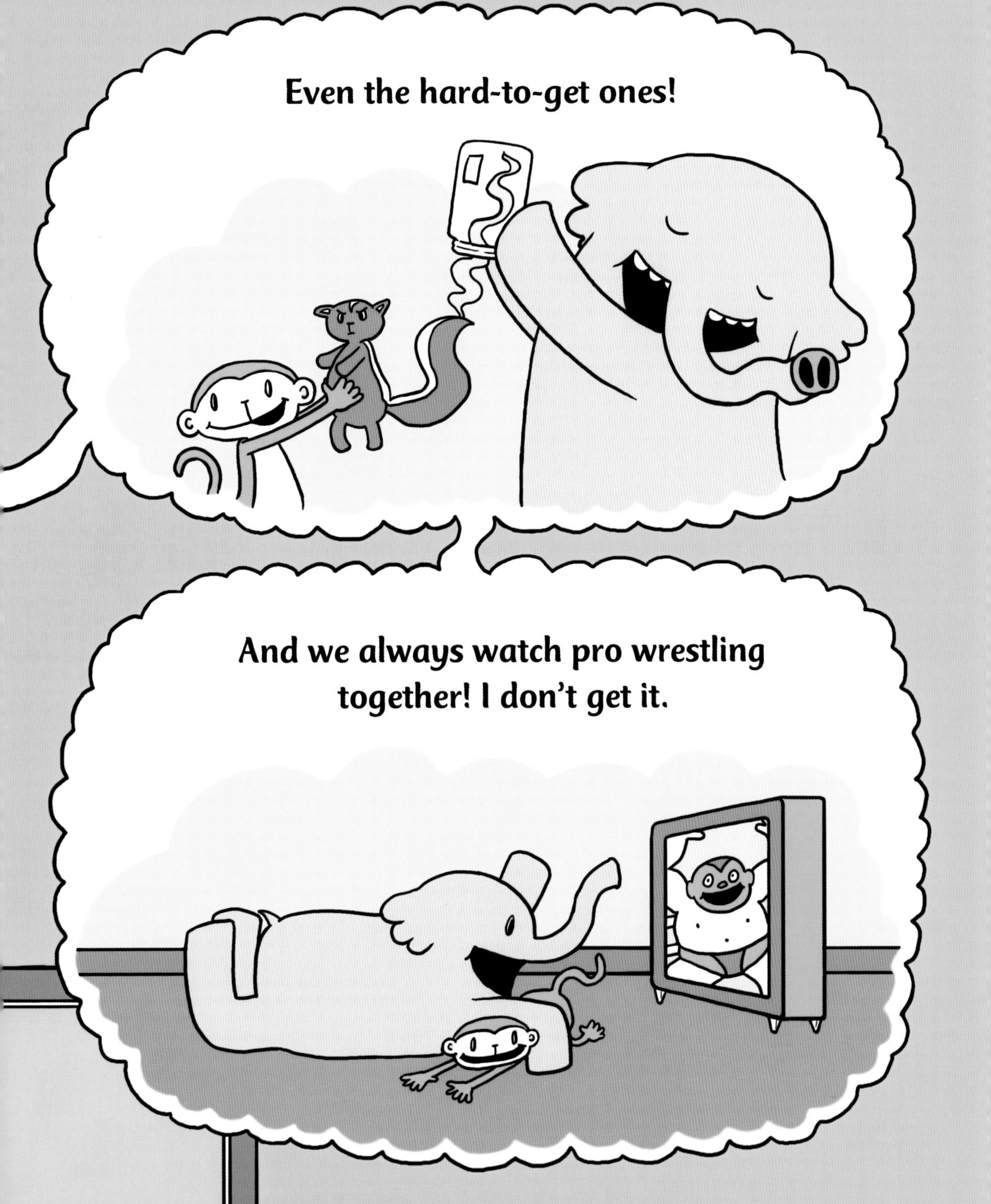
Even the hard-to-get ones!
And we always watch pro wrestling together! I don't get it.

Then Elephant got mad too.

He decided to get even by giving the Bunny family the keys to Monkey's house.

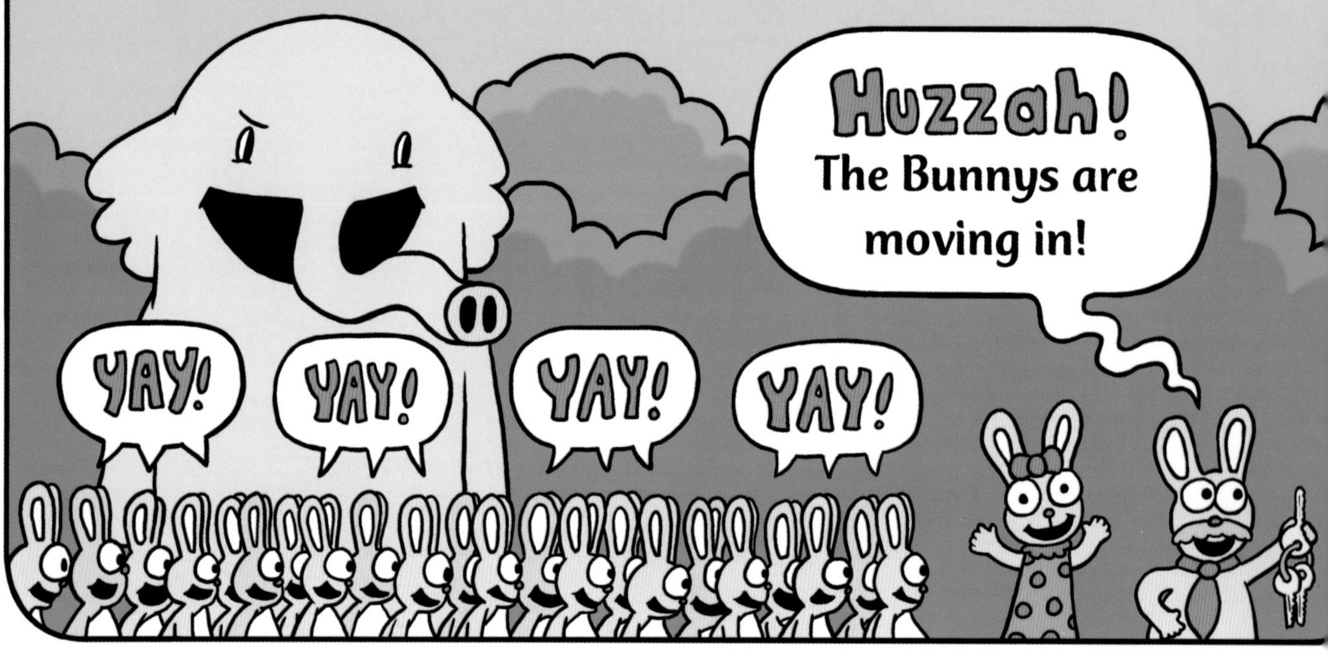
Huzzah!
The Bunnys are moving in!
YAY!
YAY!
YAY!
YAY!

Monkey retaliated by painting a face on Elephant as he took a nap.

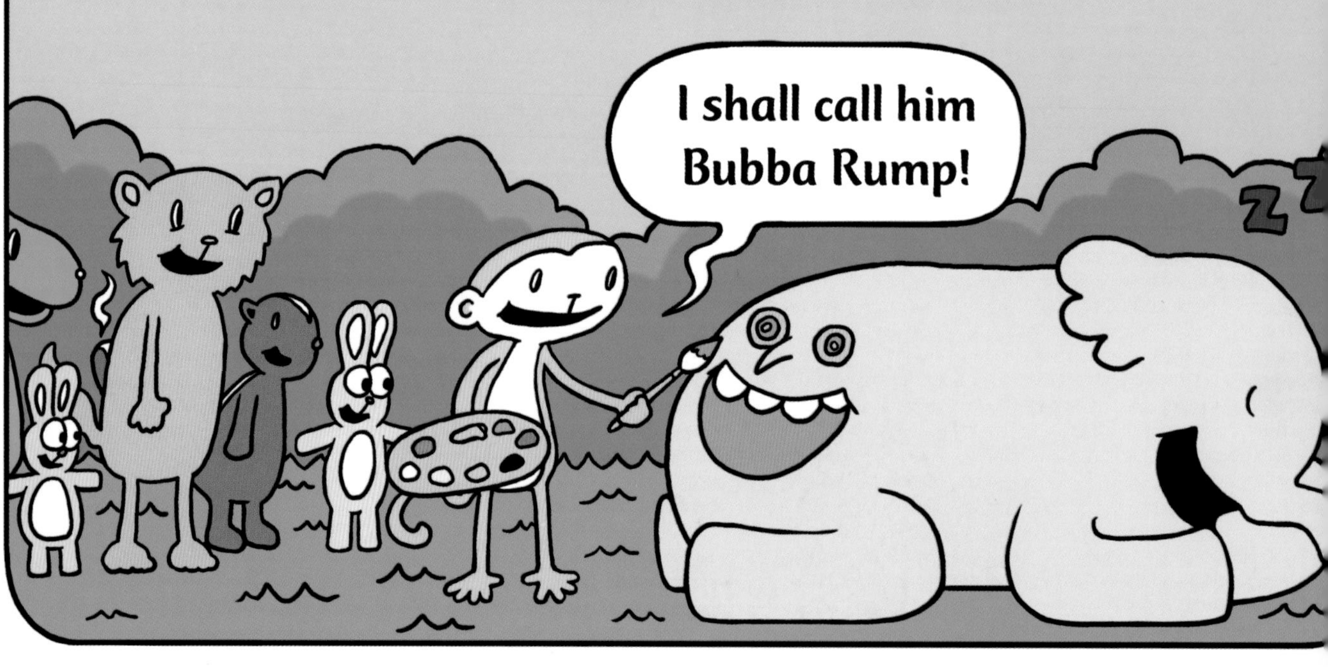
I shall call him Bubba Rump!

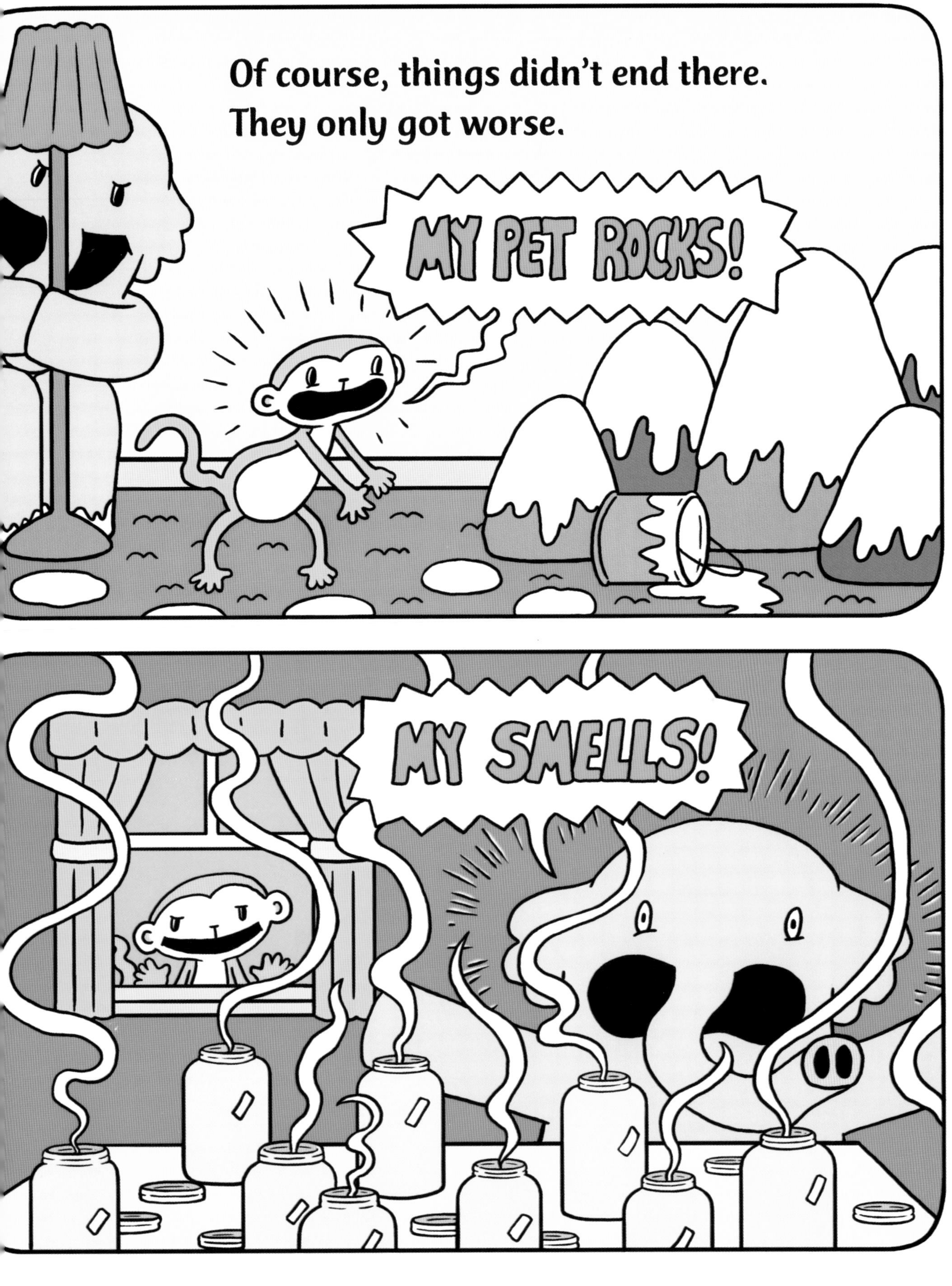
Of course, things didn't end there.
They only got worse.
MY PET ROCKS!
MY SMELLS!

Eventually, an all out war developed.

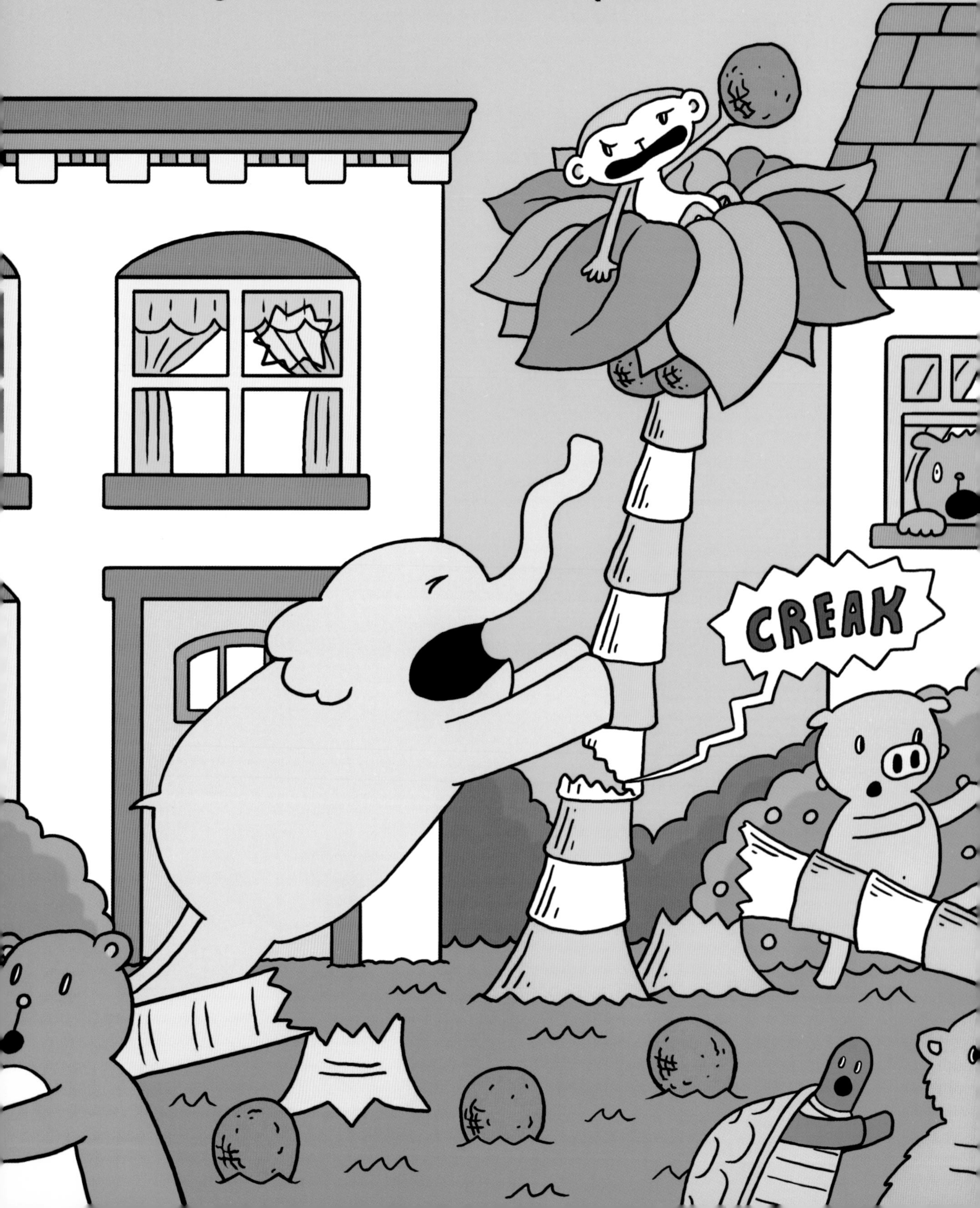
CREAK

Nobody knew exactly what had happened, but they did know the Island was becoming a very un-safe place.

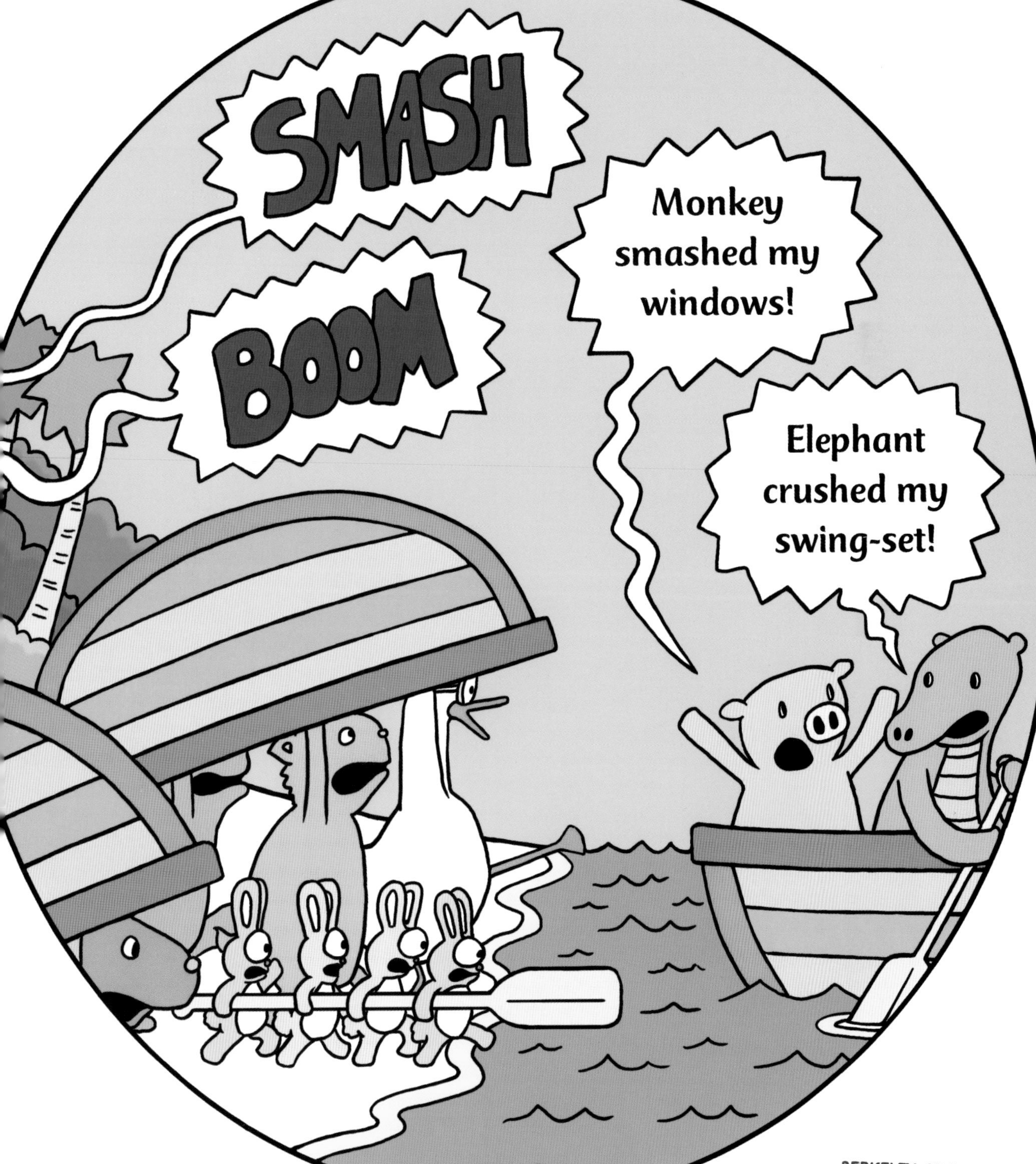
SMASH
BOOM
Monkey smashed my windows!
Elephant crushed my swing-set!

Something had to be done. Many ideas were put forth, but none were very good.

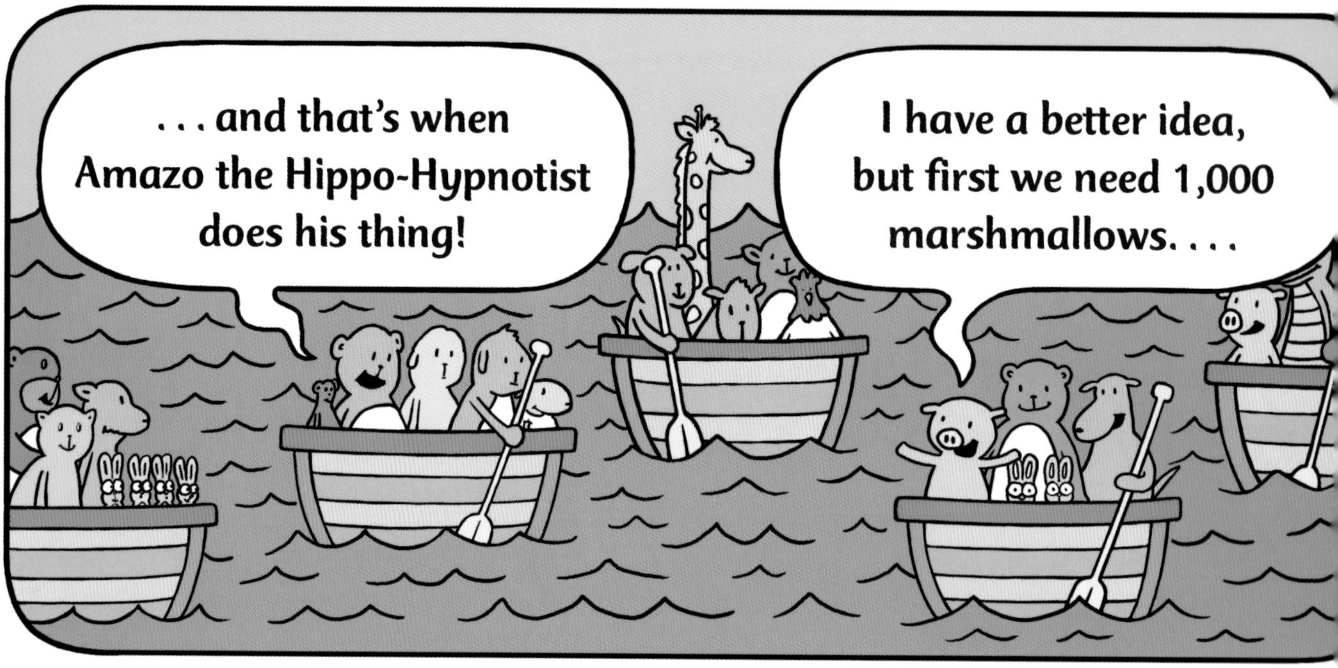
. . . and that's when Amazo the Hippo-Hypnotist does his thing!
I have a better idea, but first we need 1,000 marshmallows. . . .

Eventually, Professor Duck came up with a great one! Massive planning ensued.

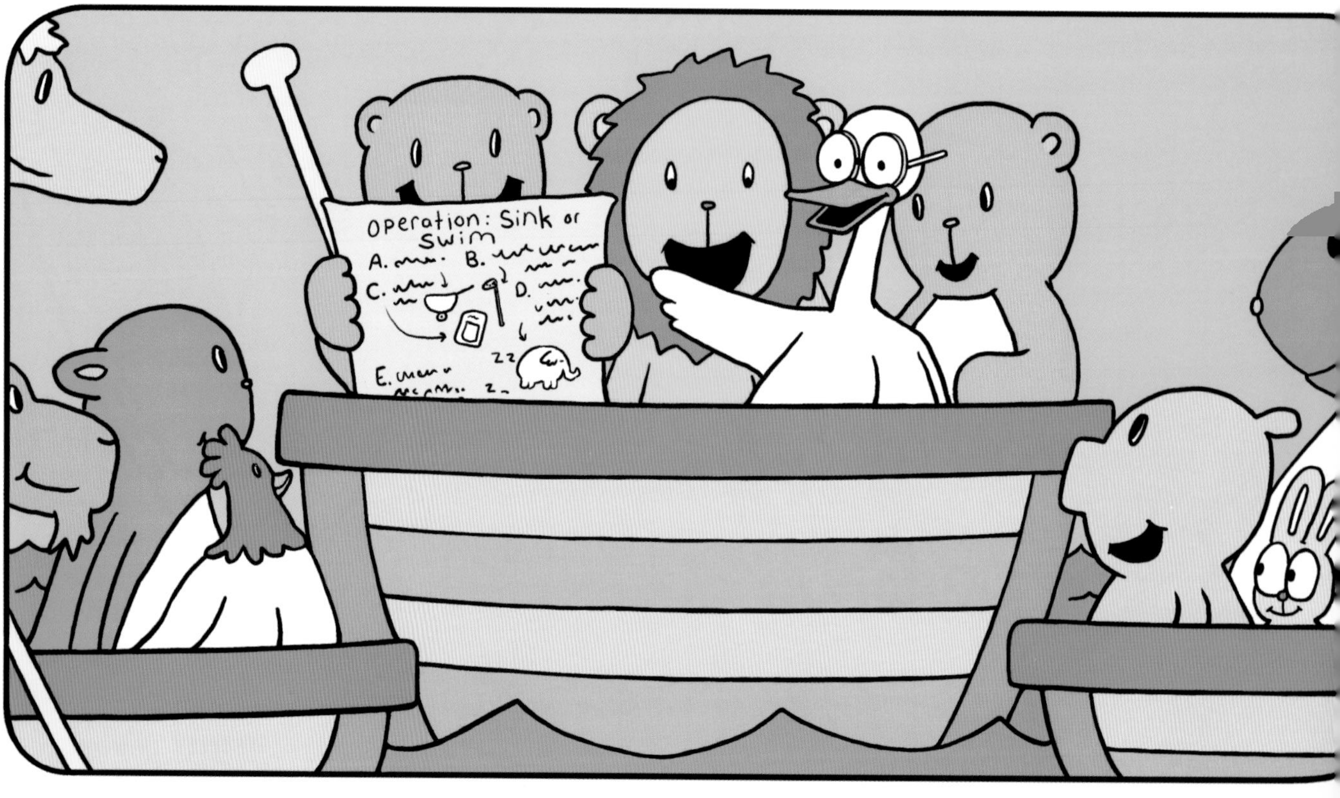
Operation: Sink or Swim
A.
B.
C.
D.
E.

Later that night, Operation: Sink or Swim was launched.

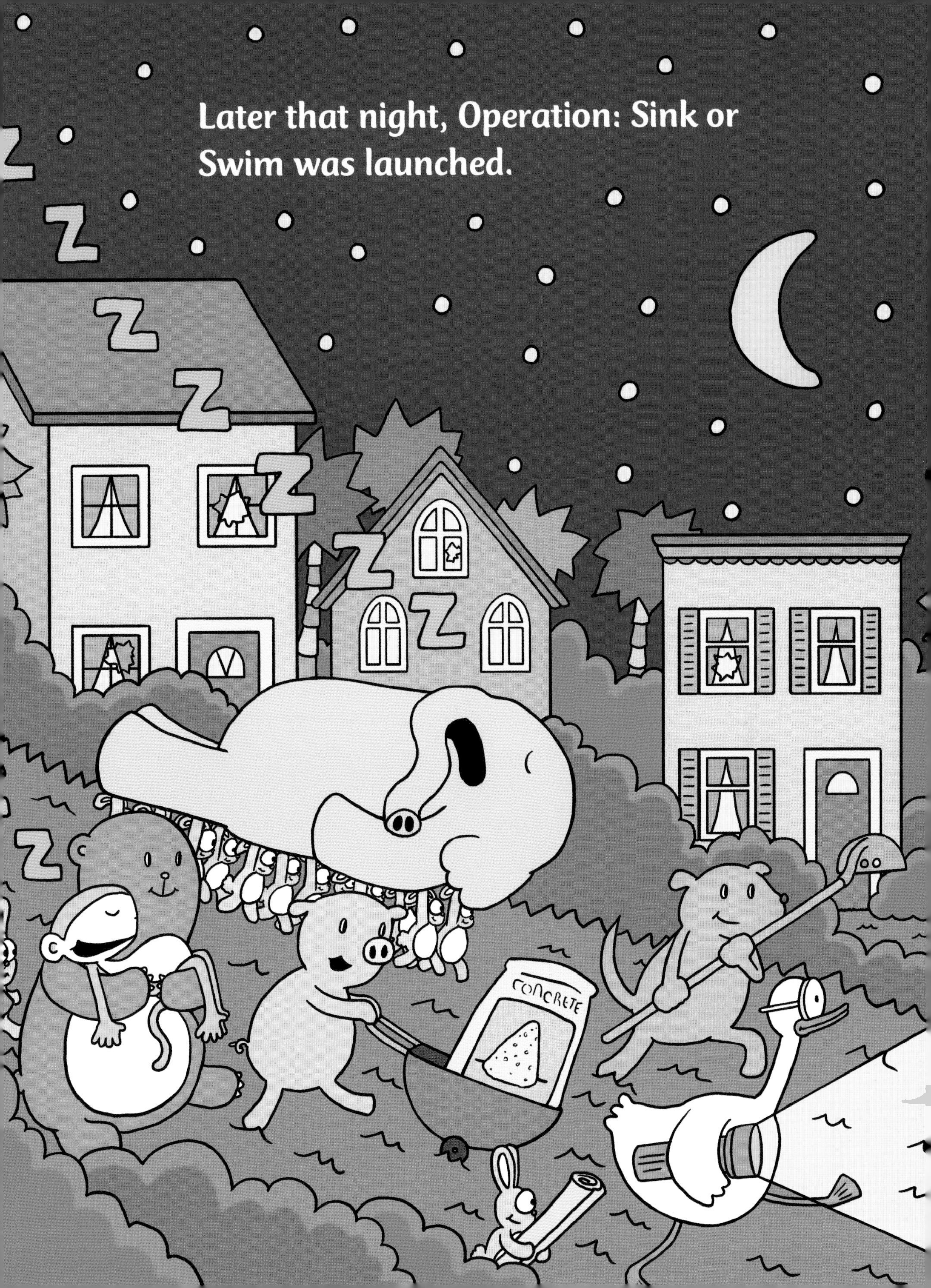
CONCRETE

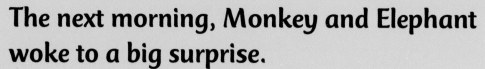

The next morning, Monkey and Elephant
woke to a big surprise.

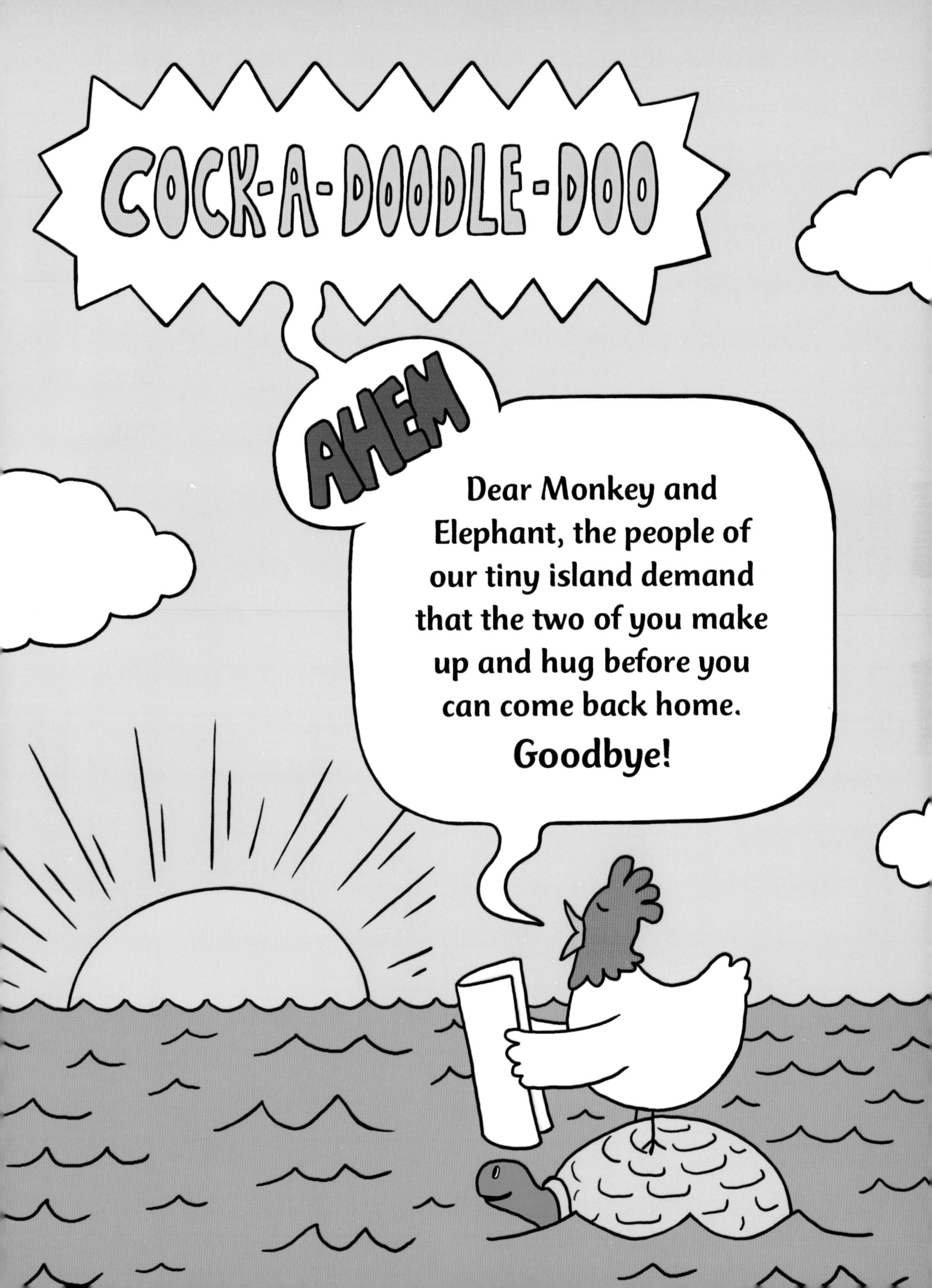
COCK-A-DOODLE-DOO
AHEM
Dear Monkey and Elephant, the people of our tiny island demand that the two of you make up and hug before you can come back home.
Goodbye!

Elephant, who was an excellent swimmer, was all set to swim back when . . .

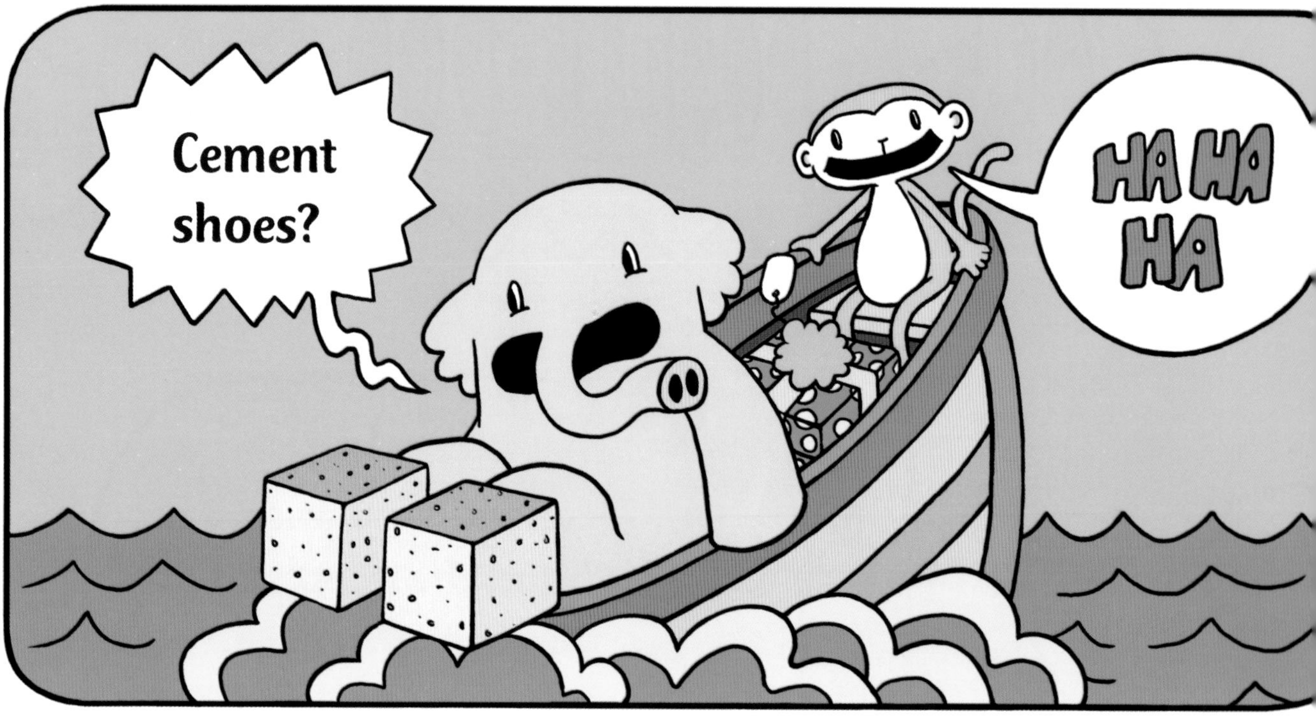
Cement shoes?
HA HA HA

Monkey, who could not swim, found a gift with his name on it.

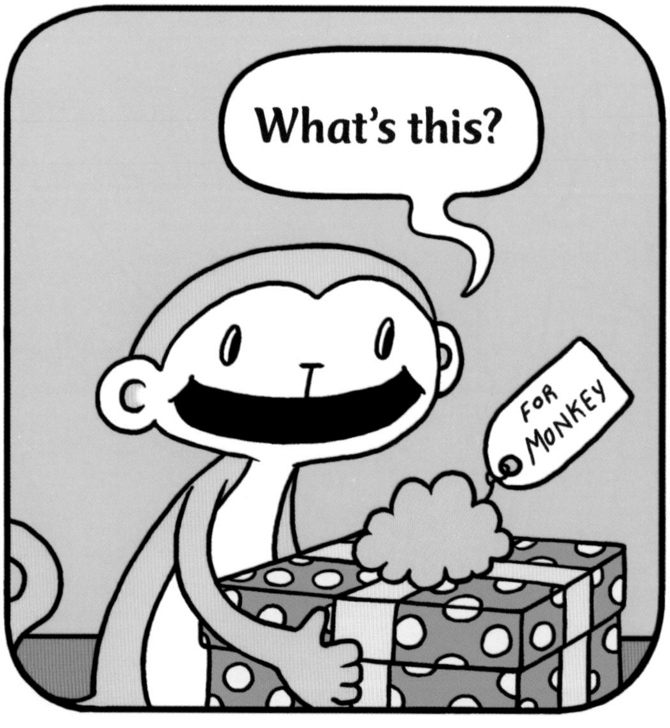
What's this?
FOR MONKEY

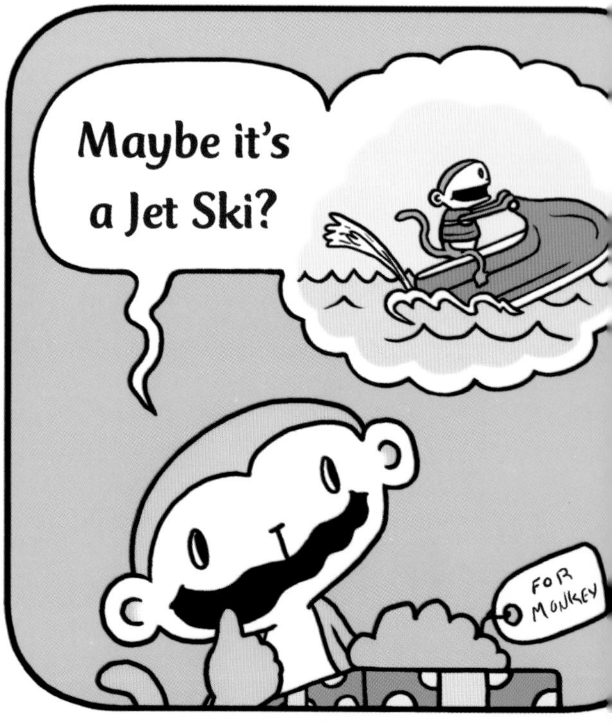
Maybe it's a Jet Ski?
FOR MONKEY

It was not a Jet Ski.

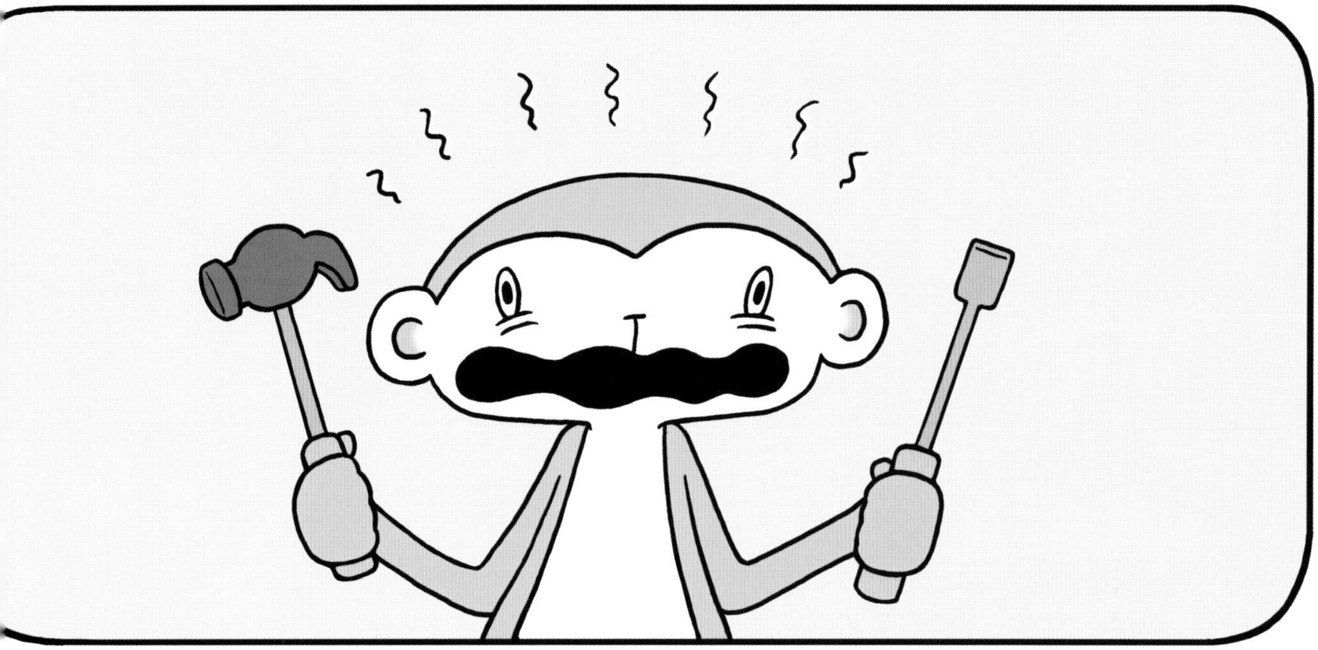

Monkey had no need for a hammer and chisel,
but he did not want to share his gift with Elephant.

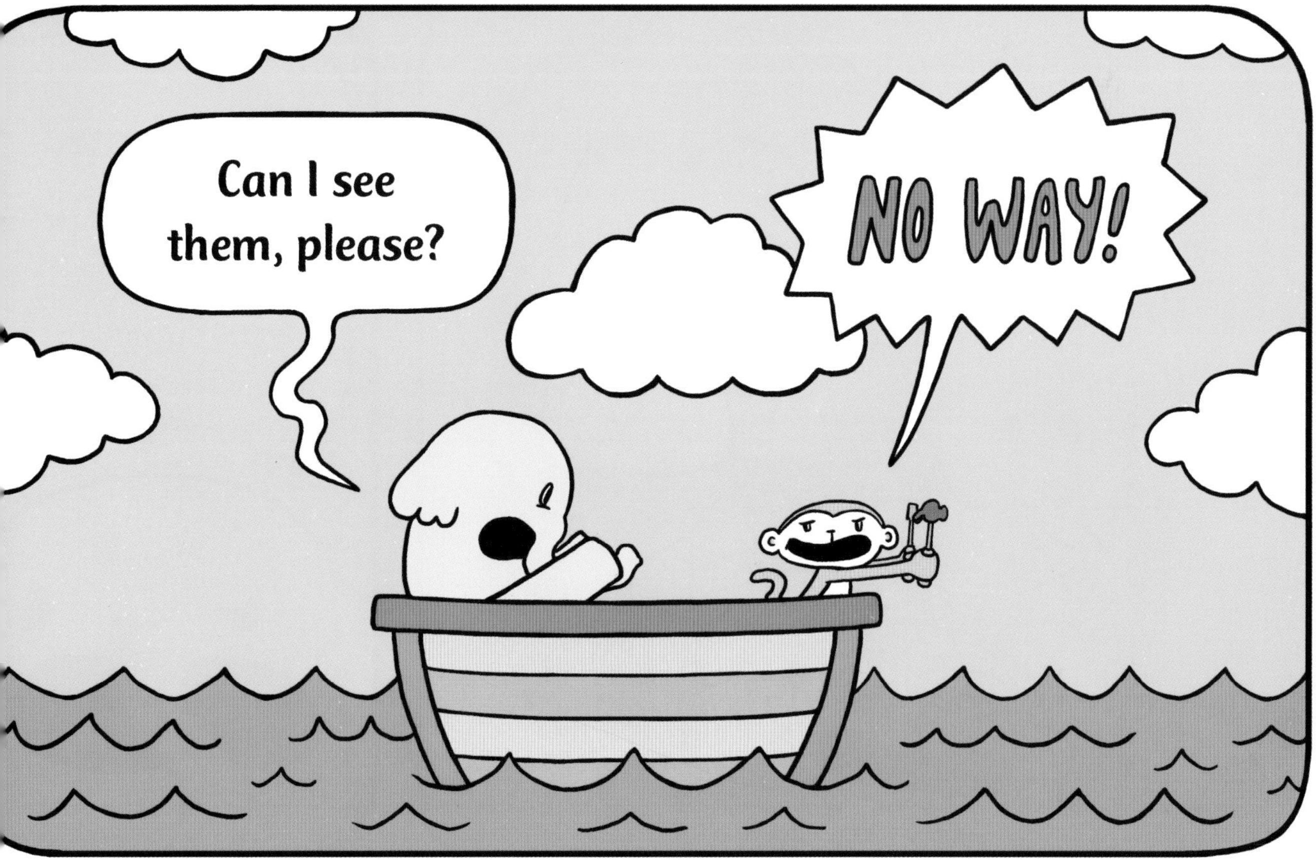
Can I see them, please?
NO WAY!

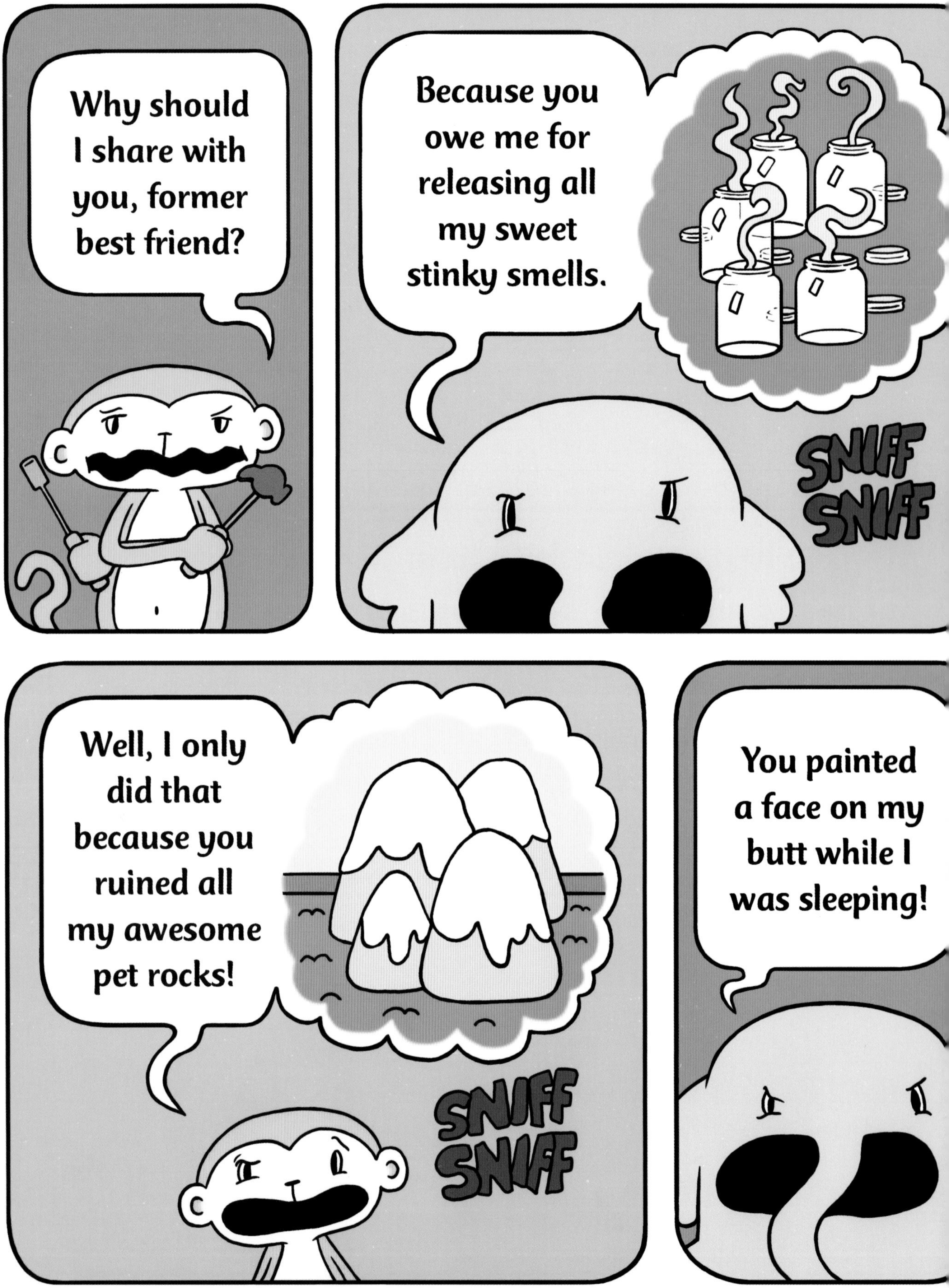
Why should I share with you, former best friend?
Because you owe me for releasing all my sweet stinky smells.
SNIFF SNIFF
Well, I only did that because you ruined all my awesome pet rocks!
SNIFF SNIFF
You painted a face on my butt while I was sleeping!

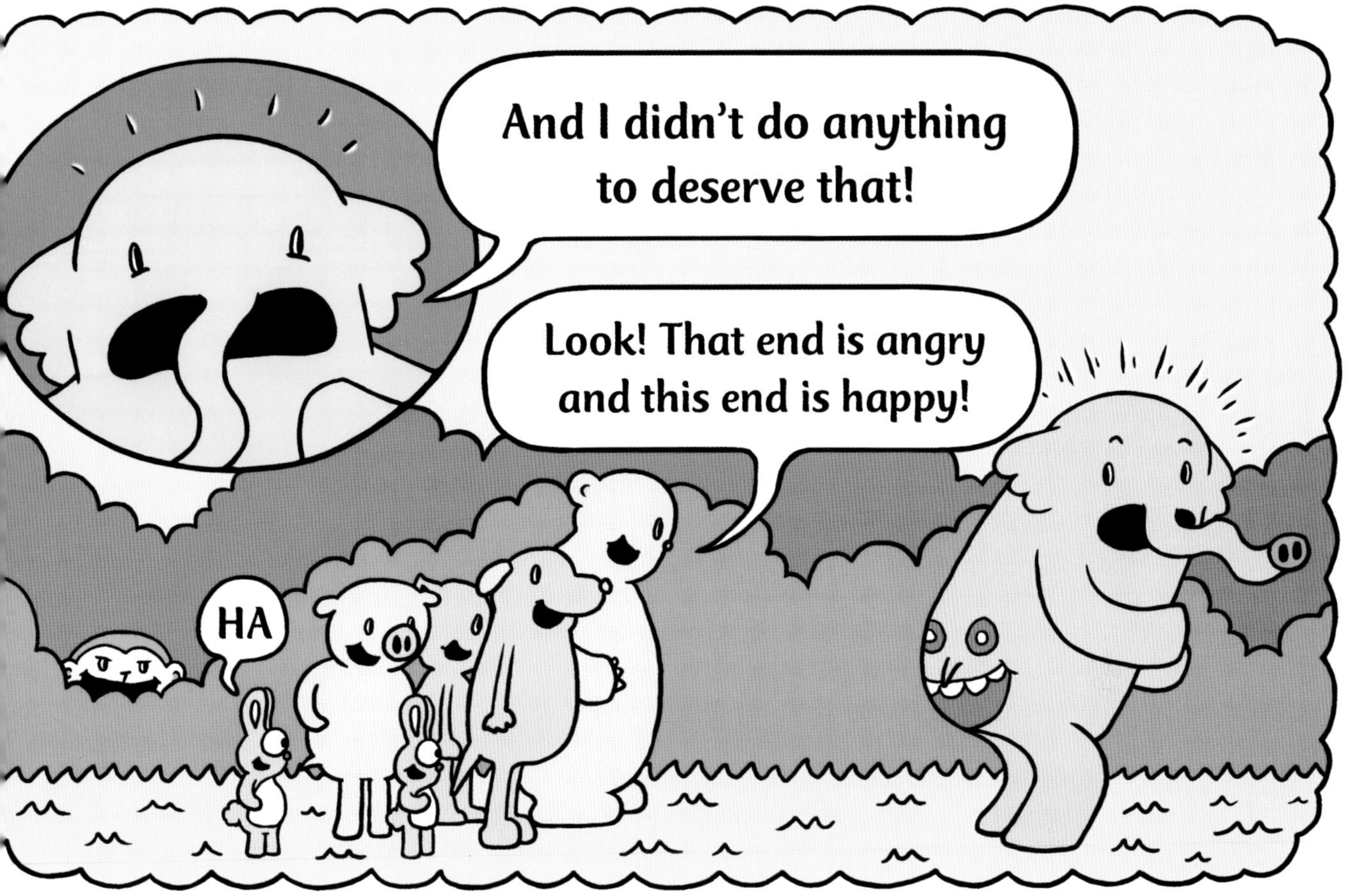
And I didn't do anything
to deserve that!
Look! That end is angry
and this end is happy!
HA

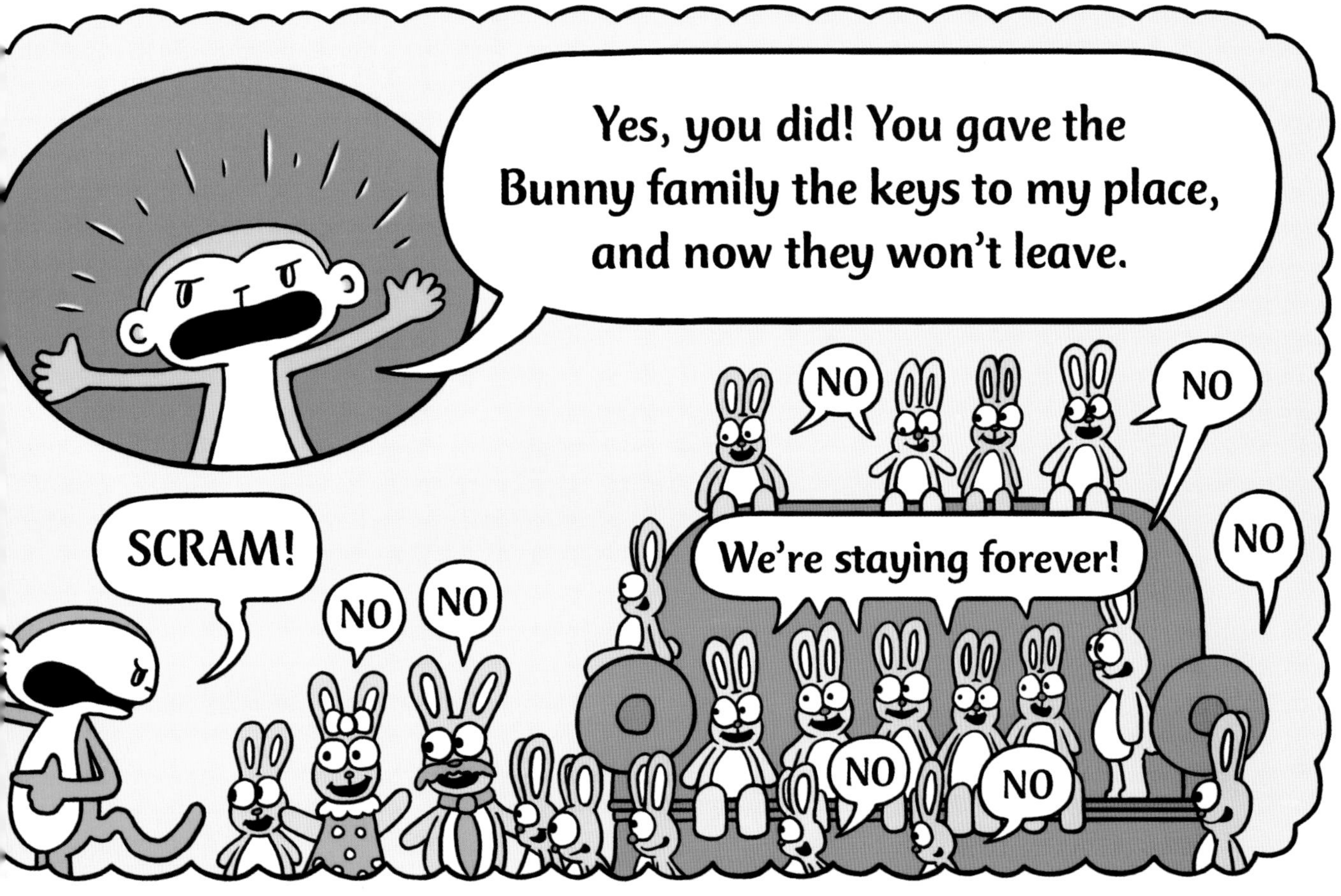
Yes, you did! You gave the
Bunny family the keys to my place,
and now they won't leave.
SCRAM!
NO
NO
NO
NO
We're staying forever!
NO
NO
NO
NO

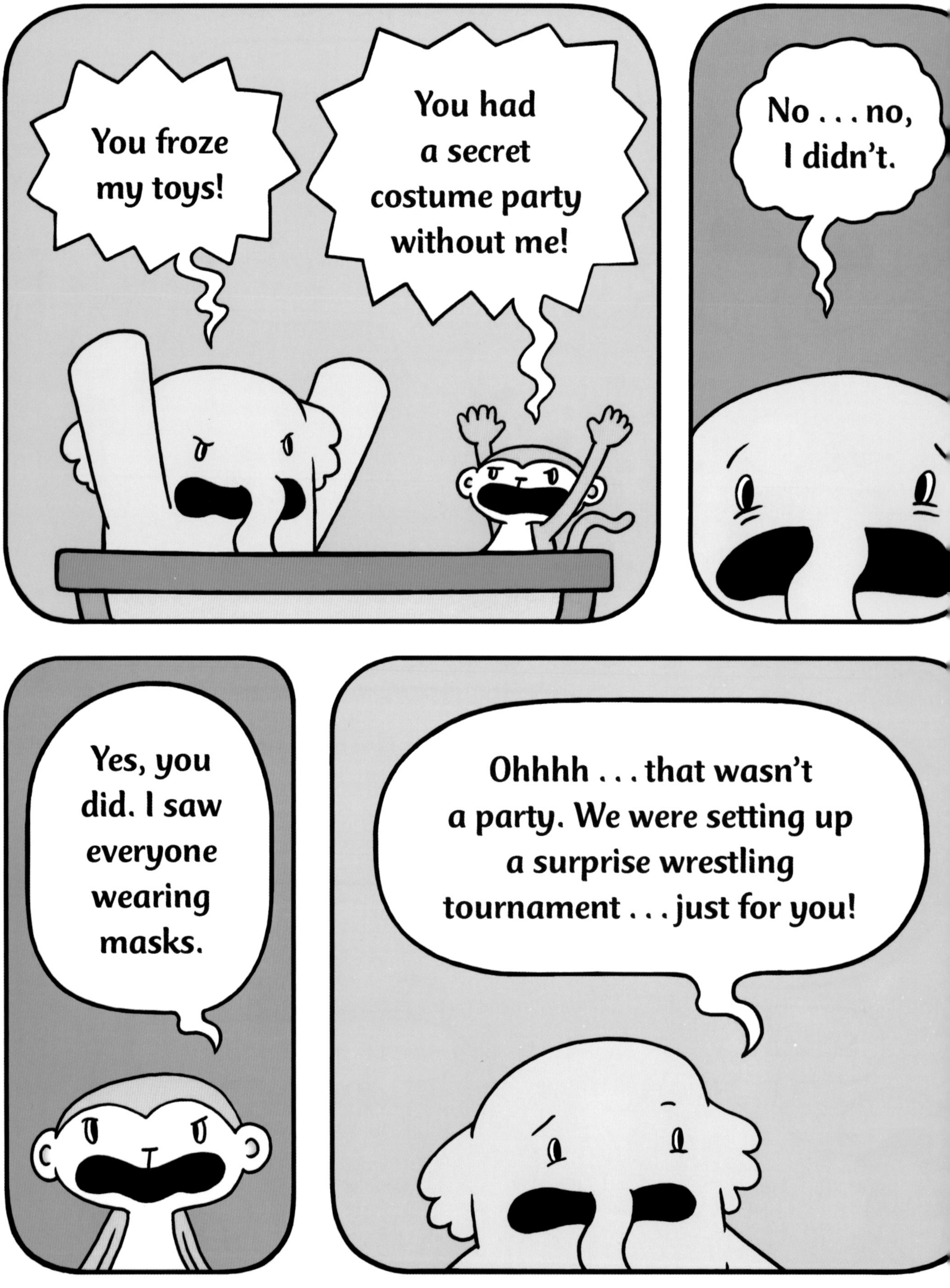
You froze my toys!
You had a secret costume party without me!
No . . . no, I didn't.
Yes, you did. I saw everyone wearing masks.
Ohhhh . . . that wasn't a party. We were setting up a surprise wrestling tournament . . . just for you!

Monkey was *sooo* embarrassed!

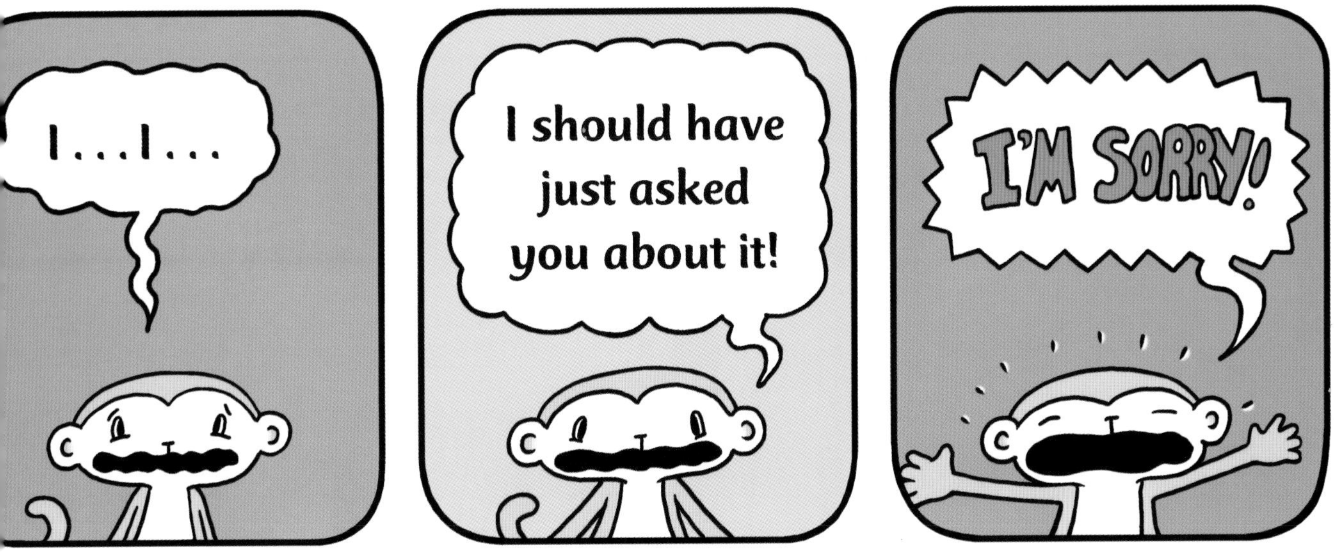
I...I...
I should have just asked you about it!
I'M SORRY!

Elephant felt bad too.

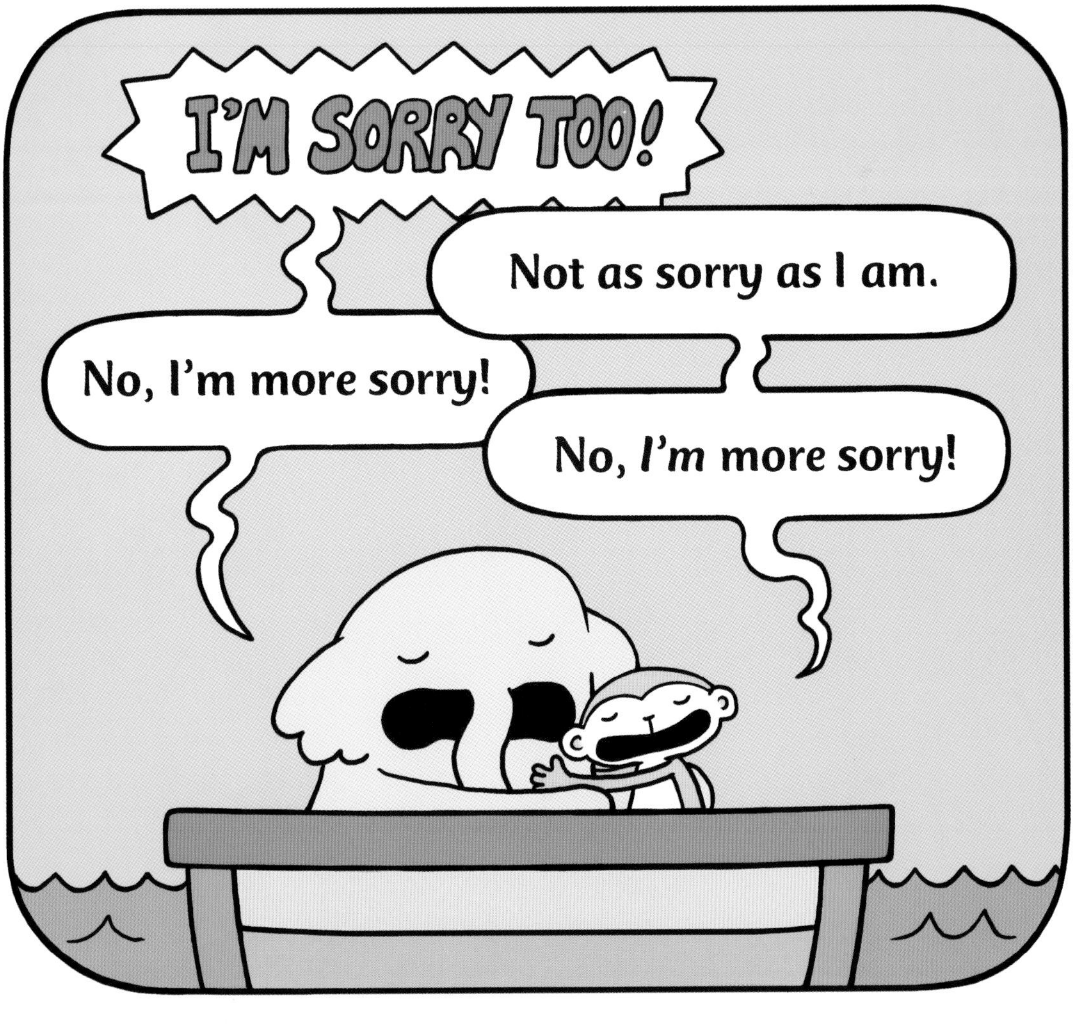
I'M SORRY TOO!
Not as sorry as I am.
No, I'm more sorry!
No, *I'm* more sorry!

When the apologies and hugs ended, Monkey and Elephant worked together and made their way home.

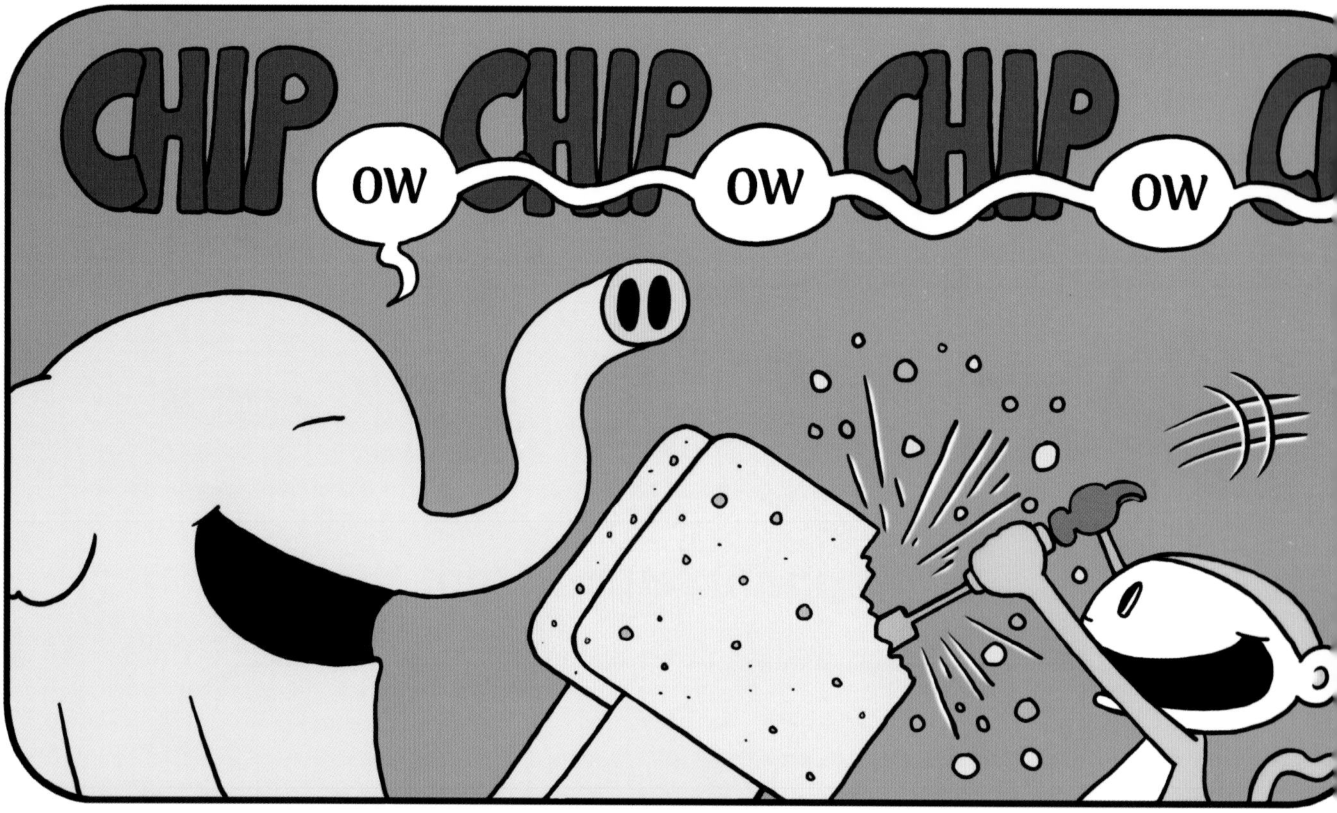
CHIP
OW
CHIP
OW
CHIP
OW

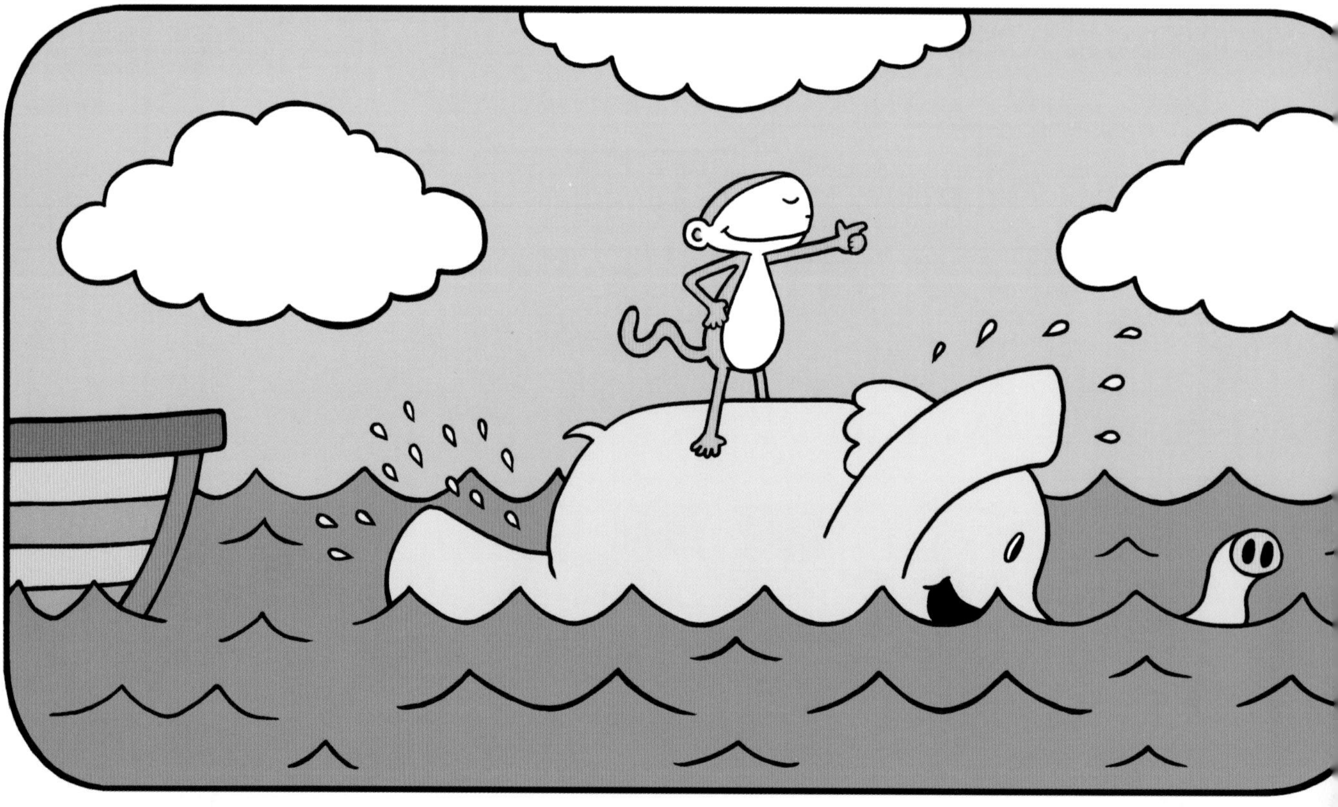

Everyone was happy to see them return.

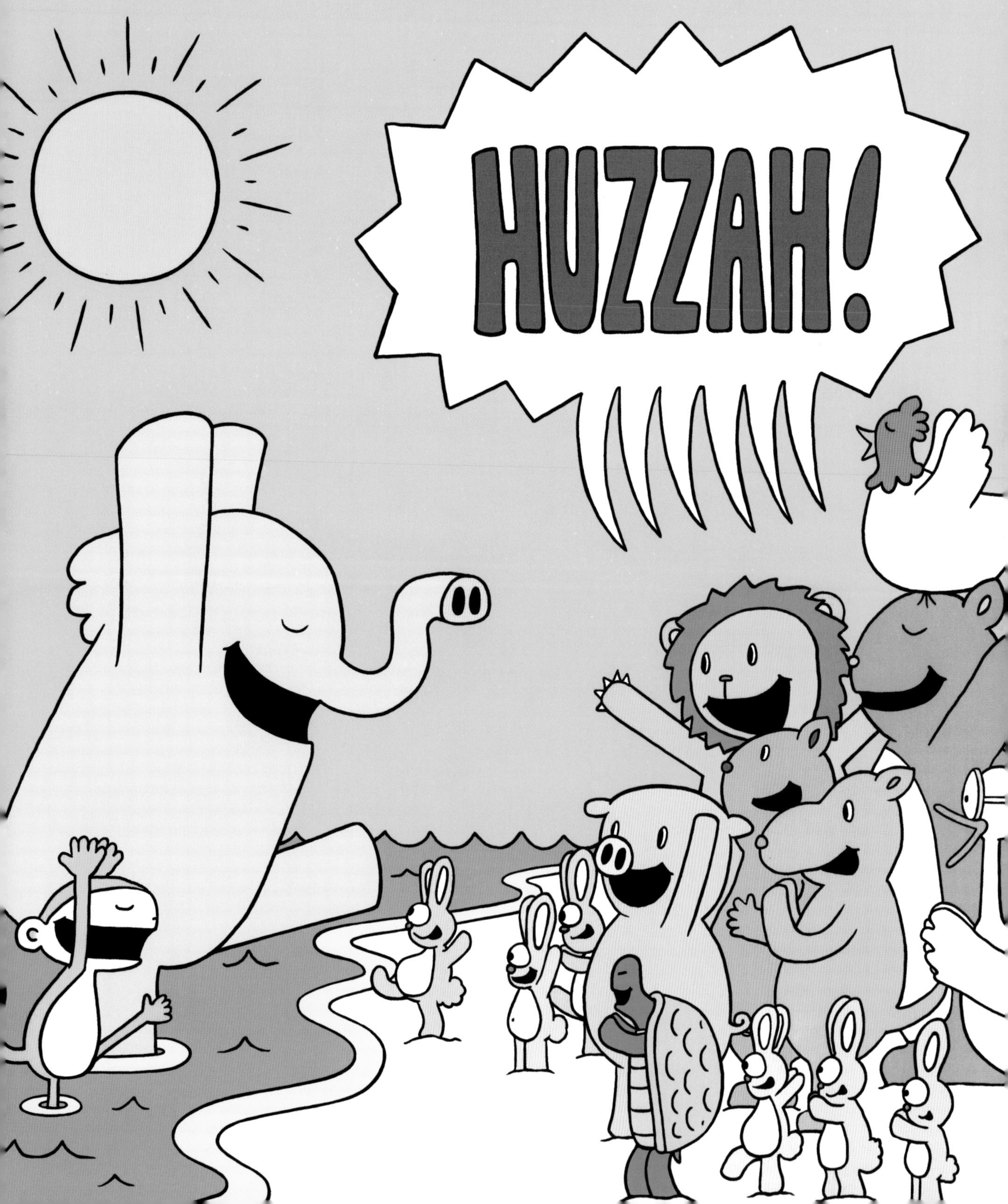
HUZZAH!

They were even happier after Monkey and Elephant fixed everything they had broken.

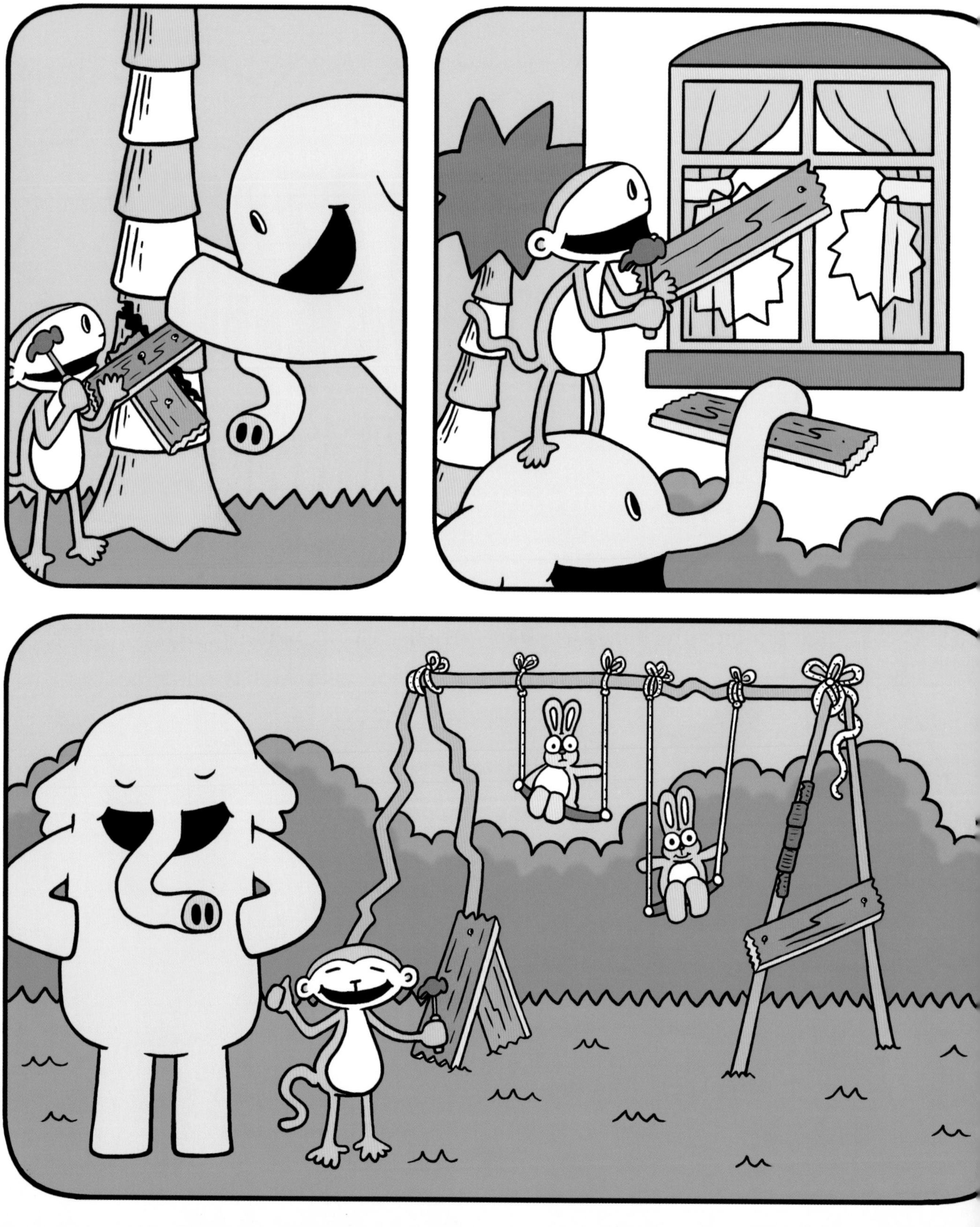

Later that night, the "not so surprise" wrestling tournament took place!

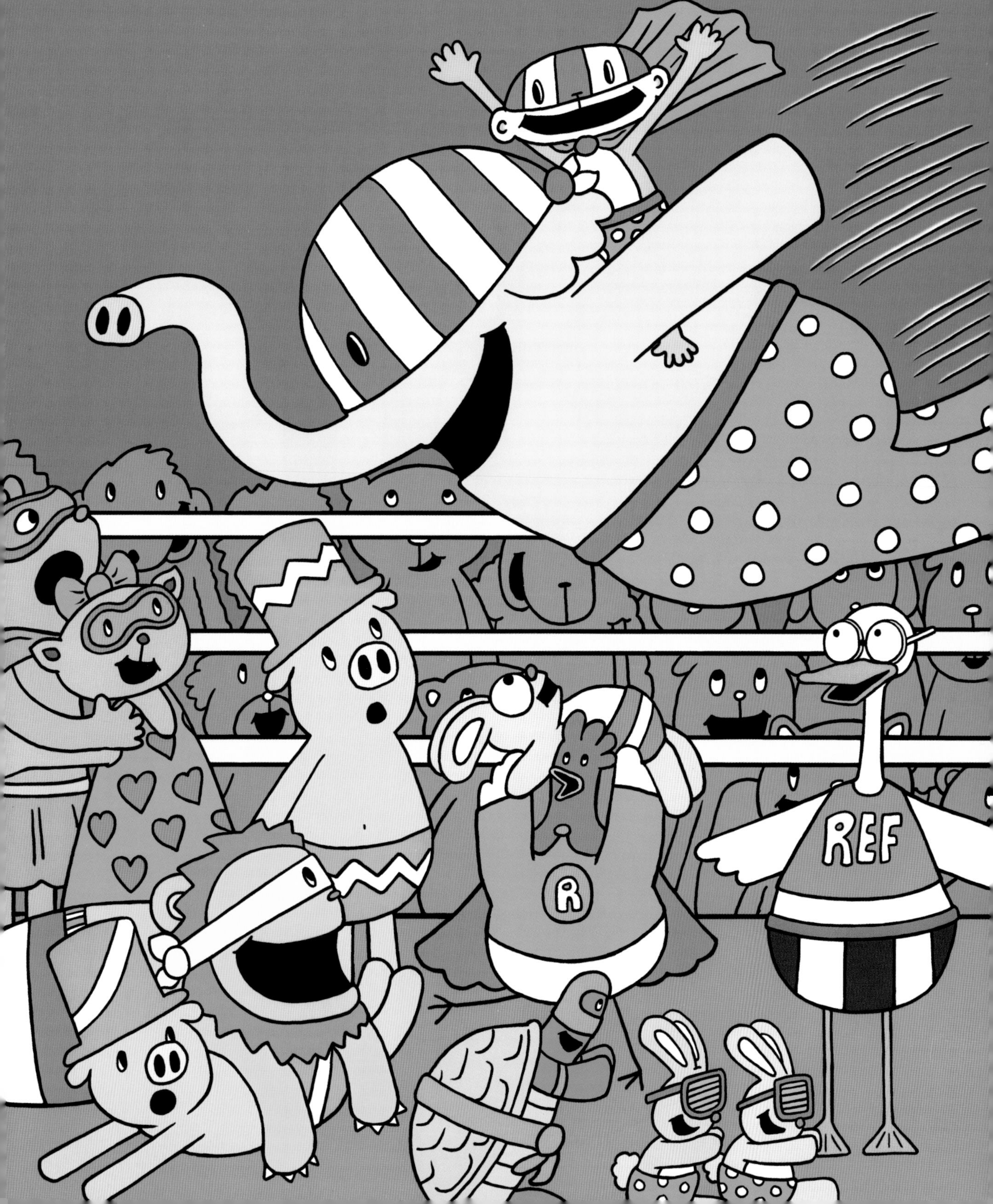
R
REF

Monkey and Elephant made the best team ever!

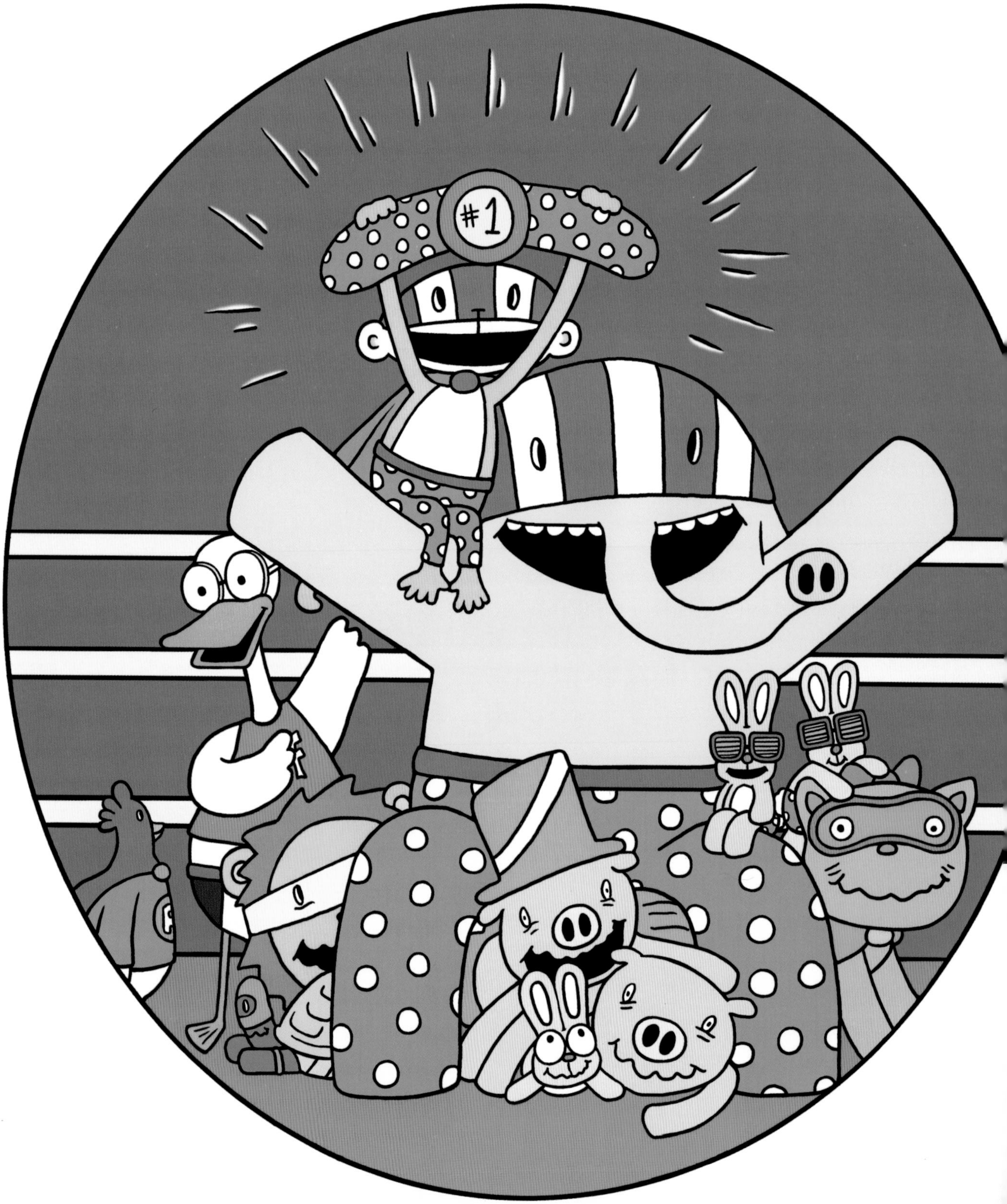
#1

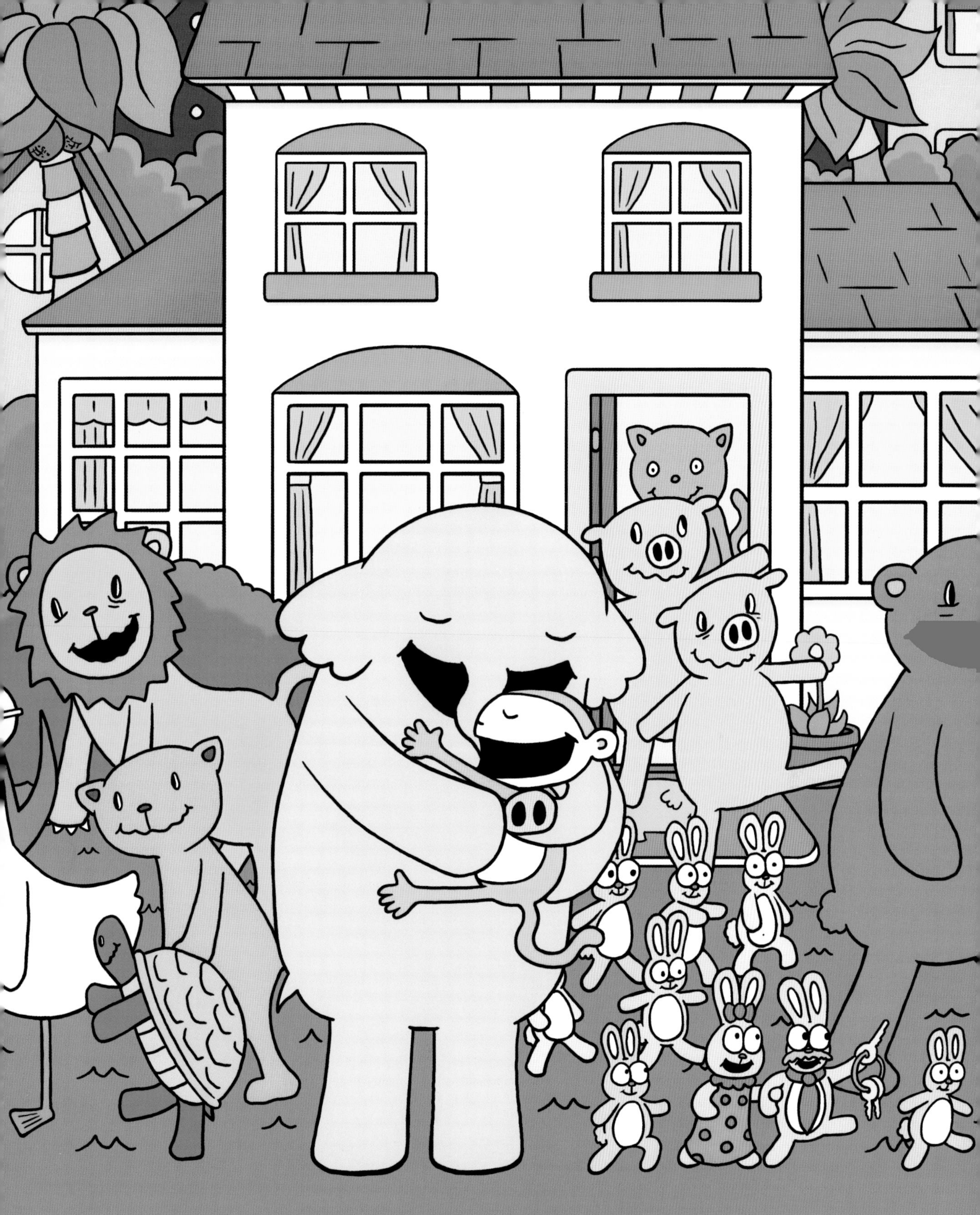

Finally, things were back to normal on the tiny island.

Well . . . almost back to normal.

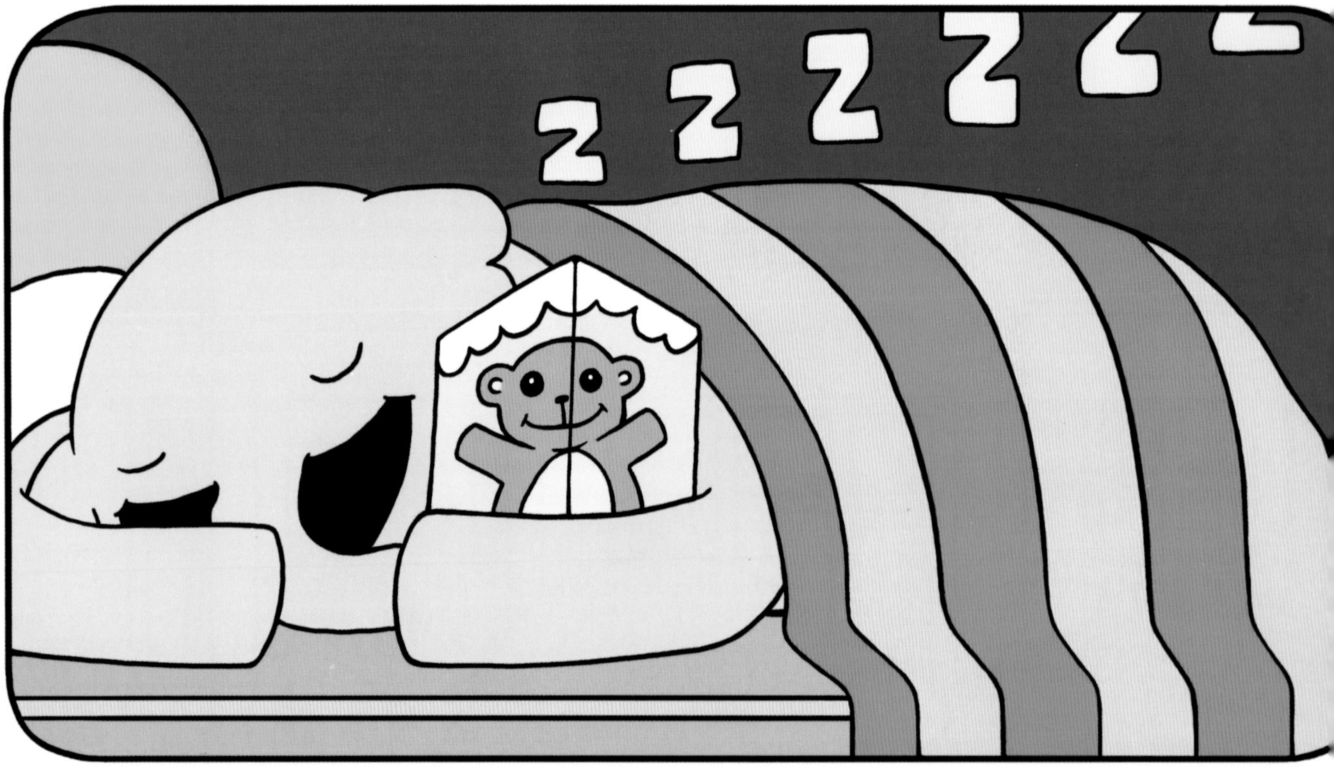

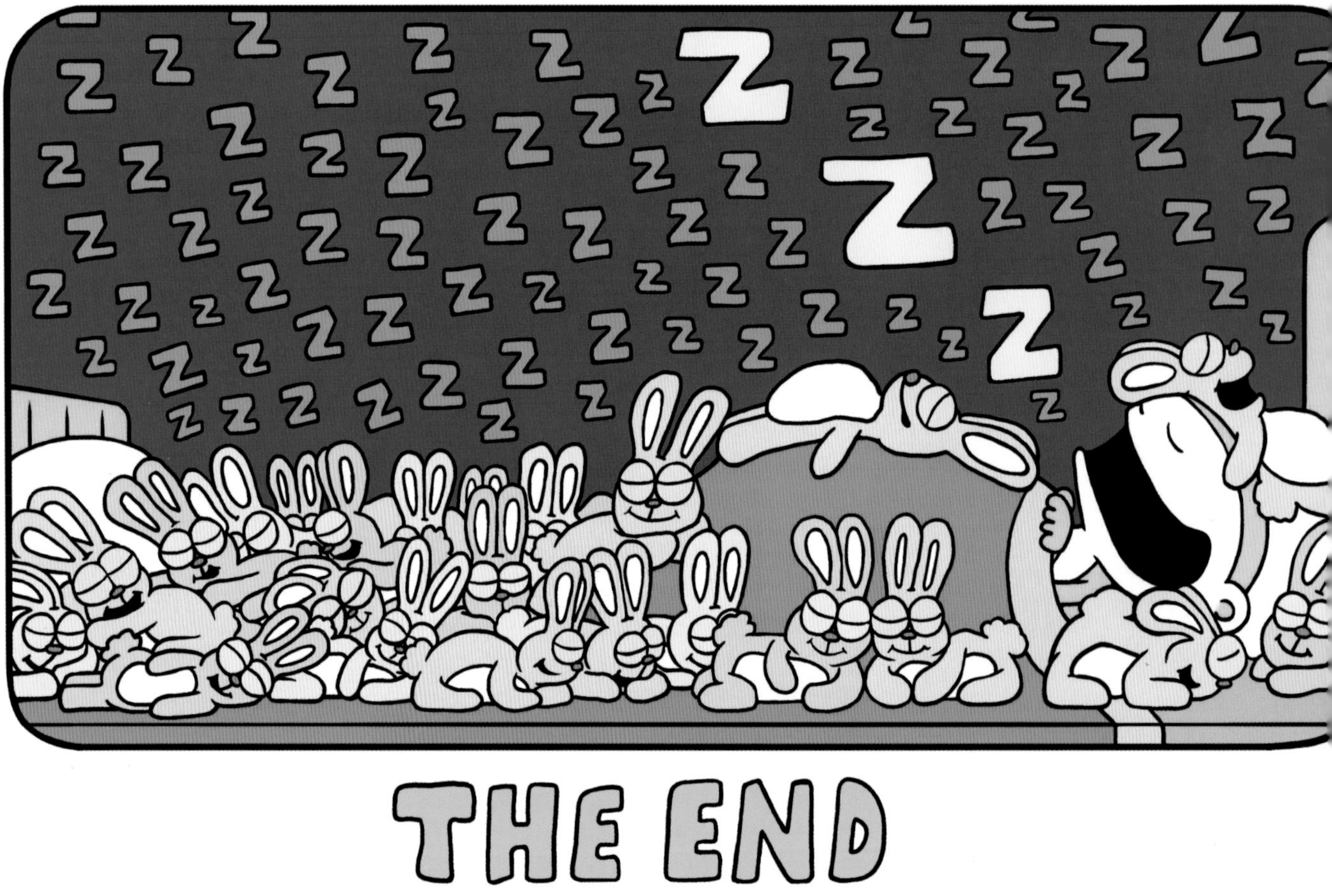

THE END